John Benson Rose

Fables of John Gay

(somewhat altered)

John Benson Rose

Fables of John Gay
(somewhat altered)

ISBN/EAN: 9783744784856

Printed in Europe, USA, Canada, Australia, Japan

Cover: Foto ©Andreas Hilbeck / pixelio.de

More available books at **www.hansebooks.com**

FABLES OF JOHN GAY

(SOMEWHAT ALTERED).

AFFECTIONATELY PRESENTED TO

MARGARET ROSE,

BY HER UNCLE

JOHN BENSON ROSE.

[*FOR PRIVATE CIRCULATION.*]

LONDON:

PRINTED BY WILLIAM CLOWES & SONS, STAMFORD STREET,
AND CHARING CROSS.

1871.

DEDICATION.

Sí doulce la Margarite.

WHEN I first saw you—never mind the year—you could speak no English, and when next I saw you, after a lapse of two years, you *would* prattle no French; when again we met, you were the nymph with bright and flowing hair, which frightened his Highness Prince James out of his feline senses, when, as you came in by the door, he made his bolt by the window. It was then that you entreated me, with "most petitionary vehemence," to write you a book—a big book—thick, and all for yourself—

> " Apollo heard, and granting half the prayer,
>   Shuffled to winds the rest and tossed in air."

I have not written the book, nor is it thick: but I have printed you a book, and it is thin. And I take the occasion to note that old Geoffry Chaucer, our father poet, must have had you in his mind's eye, by prescience or precognition, or he could hardly else have written two poems, one on the daisy and one on the rose. They are poems too long for modern days, nor are we equal in patience to our forefathers, who read ' The Faërie Queen,' 'Gondibert,' and the ' Polyolbion,' annually, as they cheeringly averred, *through and out.* Photography, steam, and electricity make us otherwise, and Patience has fled to the spheres; therefore, if feasible, shall " brevity be the soul of wit," and we will eschew "tediousness and outward flourishes" in compressing 'The Flower and the Leaf' into little :—

The Flower and the Leaf.

A maiden in greenwood in month of sweet May,
Arose and awoke at the dawn of the day :
    As she wended along,
    She heard fairie song—
"𝔖i 𝔡oulce est la 𝔐argarite."
There the Ladye the Flower and Ladye the Leaf,
With knights and squires of fairie chief,
    Were met upon mead,
    For devoir and deed—
Homage unto "𝔏a 𝔡oulce 𝔐argarite."

There the ladye in white and the ladye in green
Sat on their thrones by the Fairie Queen,
    Whilst knights did their duty,
    And bowed down to beauty—
"𝔖i 𝔡oulce est la 𝔐argarite,"—
When the skies grew hot and the ladies pale,
And the storm descended in lightning and hail,
    As they danced and sung,
    And the burden rung—
"𝔖ous la feuille, sous la feuille, meet."

Our Ladye of Leaf asked her of the Flower
And fairie Nymphs to shelter in bower :
    And they danced and sung,
    And the refrain rung—
"𝔖i 𝔡oulce est la 𝔐argarite."
All woe begone shivered the Ladye Flower,
The Ladye Leaf glittered in gems from the shower :
    As they danced and sung,
    And the refrain rung—
"𝔖i 𝔡oulce est la 𝔐argarite."

And knights and squires then wended forth,
East and west, and south and north :
  To free forests and shores
  From giants and boars,
And shelter in night and in storm;
And every knight bore *in chief* on his shield
The *foyle en verte* on an *argent* field :
  And they rode and they sung
  The huge oaks among :—
" 𝕾𝖔𝖚𝖘 𝖑𝖆 𝖋𝖊𝖚𝖎𝖑𝖑𝖊, 𝖘𝖔𝖚𝖘 𝖑𝖆 𝖋𝖊𝖚𝖎𝖑𝖑𝖊, 𝖉𝖔𝖗𝖒𝖊."

The maiden then asked of the Fairie Queen
To tell her the moral of what she had seen :
  Who answered and sung
  In her fairie tongue—
" 𝕾𝖎 𝖉𝖔𝖚𝖑𝖈𝖊 𝖊𝖘𝖙 𝖑𝖆 𝕸𝖆𝖗𝖌𝖆𝖗𝖎𝖙𝖊."
The knight that is wise will lead from bower
The lasting Leaf—not the fading Flower :
  And when storms arise
  To turmoil life's skies—
" 𝕾𝖔𝖚𝖘 𝖑𝖆 𝖋𝖊𝖚𝖎𝖑𝖑𝖊, 𝖘𝖔𝖚𝖘 𝖑𝖆 𝖋𝖊𝖚𝖎𝖑𝖑𝖊, 𝖒𝖊𝖊𝖙."

Romaunt of the Rose.

WITHIN my twentie yeares of age,
When Love asserteth most his courage,
I dreamed a dream, now fain to tell—
A dream that pleased me wondrous well.
Now this dream will I rime aright,
To make your heartes gaye and light;
For Love desireth it—also
Commandeth me that it be so.
It is the Romaunt of the Rose,
And tale of love I must disclose.

Fair is the matter for to make,
But fairer—if she will to take
For whom the romaunt is begonne
For that I wis she is the fair one
Of mokle prise; and therefore she
So worthier is beloved to be;
And well she ought of prise and right
Be clepened Rose of every wight.
But it was May, thus dreamed me,—
A time of love and jollitie:
A time there is no husks or straw,
But new grene leaves on everie shaw;
The woods were grene, the earth was proud,
Beastès and birdès sung aloud;
And earth her poore estate forgote,
In which the winter her had fraught.
Ah! ben in May the sunne is bright,
And everie thing does take delight:
The nightingale then singeth blithe;
Then is blissful many a scithe;
The goldfinch and the popinjay,
They then have many things to say.
Hard is his heart that loveth nought
In May, when all such love is wrought.
  Right from my bed full readilie,
That it was by the morrow earlie;
And up I rose, and gan me clothe
Anon I with my handès bothe:
A silver needle forth I drew
Out of an aguiler quainte inew,
And gan this needle threade anone,
For out of town me list to gone,

Jollife and gaye, full of gladnesse,
Towards a river gan I me dresse,
For from a hill that stood there neere
Came down the stream of that rivere—
My face, I wis, there saw I wele,
The bottom ypaved everie dele
With gravel, which was shining shene,
In meadows soft and soote and greene.
And full attempre out of drede
Then gan I walken throw the mede
Downward ever in my playing
As the river's waters straying;
And when I had awhile igone
I saw a garden right anone,
Of walls with many portraitures,
And bothe of images and peintures—
But you may read it as it flows
In Chaucer's Romaunt of the Rose.

Chaucer to his Booke.

Now go, my booke, and be courageous,
  For now I send you forthe into the worlde.
And though ye may find some outrageous,
  And in a pette be in some cornere hurl'd;
Yet you by little fingeres will be greasèd
  And known hereafter by the marke of thumbe;
At which, my little booke, be ye well pleasèd,
  For booke, like mouthe, unopenèd is dumbe.
And there be some, perchance, will bidde you off
  To Conventrè, or Yorke, or Jericho;

But be not you, my booke, abashed by scoff,
  For I will teach you where you boun to go,—
Which is in Gloucestershire, there unto Bisley,
  Where the church spire is spièd long afarre;
It is not either uncouth, square, or grisly,
  But soareth high, as if to catch a starre;
Where shall the brother of the 𝕮𝖍𝖗𝖎𝖘𝖙𝖎𝖆𝖓 𝖄𝖊𝖆𝖗𝖊,
  𝕽𝖊𝖇𝖑𝖊, hereafter tend the seven springs,
Above whose fountains doth 𝕿𝖍𝖊 𝕲𝖗𝖔𝖛𝖊 uprear,
  Like to Mount Helicon, where Clio sings,
Where rookès build, and peacocke spreadeth tail,
  And there the wood-pigeon doth sobbe Coo coo;
Neither do sparrow, merle or mavis fail,
  And there the owl at midnight singeth Whoo.
And where there are a 𝕷𝖆𝖚𝖗𝖊𝖑 and a 𝕽𝖔𝖘𝖊,
  Beneath whose branches wide a broode doth haunt;
The whom high walls and fretted gates enclose,
  Where goode may enter, badde are bidde avaunt.
And there is one yclepen 𝕸𝖆𝖗𝖌𝖆𝖗𝖊𝖙𝖊,
  Who alsoe for the nonce is clepen Rose,
For she must on some other hille be sette
  When Hymenæos shall her lotte dispose.
And, little booke, it is to her you runne,
  And sisters eight, for they, in soothe, are nine;
And in their bowere baske as in the sunne,
  And beare 𝕸𝖆𝖎𝖉 𝕸𝖆𝖗𝖎𝖔𝖓'𝖘 love to 𝕮𝖆𝖙𝖍𝖊𝖗𝖎𝖓𝖊,
Who is her gossipe, and she is her pette;
  And nought mote save us from a wrath condign,
If you, my booke, should haplessly forgette,
  Nor bended knees, I trow, nor teares of 𝕸𝖆𝖗𝖌𝖆𝖗𝖊𝖙𝖊.

CONTENTS.

GAY'S FABLES.

INTRODUCTION.

REMOTE from cities dwelt a swain,
Unvexed by petty cares of gain;
His head was silvered, and by age
He had contented grown and sage;
In summer's heat and winter's cold
He fed his flock and penned his fold,
Devoid of envy or ambition,
So had he won a proud position.
  A deep philosopher, whose rules
Of moral life were drawn from schools,
With wonder sought this shepherd's nest,
And his perplexity expressed:
  "Whence is thy wisdom? Hath thy toil
O'er books consumed the midnight oil,
Communed o'er Greek and Roman pages,
With Plato, Socrates—those sages—
Or fathomed Tully,—or hast travelled
With wise Ulysses, and unravelled

Of customs half a mundane sphere ? ”

The shepherd answered him: “ I ne'er
From books or from mankind sought learning,
For both will cheat the most discerning;
The more perplexed the more they view
In the wide fields of false and true.

“ I draw from Nature all I know—
To virtue friend, to vice a foe.
The ceaseless labour of the bee
Prompted my soul to industry;
The wise provision of the ant
Made me for winter provident;
My trusty dog there showed the way,
And to be true I copy Tray.
Then for domestic hallowed love,
I learnt it of the cooing dove;
And love paternal followed, when
I marked devotion in the hen.

“ Nature then prompted me to school
My tongue from scorn and ridicule,
And never with important mien
In conversation to o'erween.
I learnt some lessons from the fowls:
To shun solemnity, from owls;
Another lesson from the pie,—
Pert and pretentious, and as sly;
And to detest man's raids and mulctures,
From eagles, kites, goshawks, and vultures;

But most of all abhorrence take
From the base toad or viler snake,
With filthy venom in the bite,
Of envies, jealousies, and spite.
Thus from Dame Nature and Creation
Have I deduced my observation;
Nor found I ever thing so mean,
That gave no moral thence to glean."

    Then the philosopher replied:
"Thy fame, re-echoed far and wide,
Is just and true: for books misguide,—
As full, as man himself, of pride;
But Nature, rightly studied, leads
To noble thoughts and worthy deeds."

HIS HIGHNESS WILLIAM DUKE OF CUMBERLAND.

FABLE I.

LION, TIGER, AND TRAVELLER.

ACCEPT, my Prince, the moral fable,
To youth ingenuous, profitable.
Nobility, like beauty's youth,
May seldom hear the voice of truth;
Or mark and learn the fact betimes
That flattery is the nurse of crimes.
Friendship, which seldom nears a throne,
Is by her voice of censure known.
To one in your exalted station
A courtier is a dedication;
But I dare not to dedicate
My verse e'en unto royal state.
My muse is sacred, and must teach
Truths which they slur in courtly speech.
But I need not to hide the praise,
Or veil the thoughts, a nation pays;
We in your youth and virtues trace
The dawnings of your royal race;
Discern the promptings of your breast,
Discern you succour the distrest,
Discern your strivings to attain
The heights above the lowly plain.

Thence shall Nobility inspire
Your bosom with her holy fire;
Impressing on your spirit all
Her glorious and heroical.

———

 A tigress prowling for her prey
Assailed a traveller on his way;
A passing lion thought no shame
To rob the tigress of her game.
They fought: he conquered in the strife;
Of him the traveller begged for life.
His life the generous lion gave,
And him invited to his cave.
Arrived, they sat and shared the feast.
 The lion spoke: he said, " What beast
Is strong enough to fight with me?
You saw the battle, fair and free.
My vassals fear me on my throne:
These hills and forests are my own.
The lesser tribes of wolf and bear
Regard my royal den with fear;
Their carcases, on either hand,
And bleaching bones now strew the land."
 " It is so," said the man, " I saw
What well might baser natures awe;
But shall a monarch, like to you,
Place glory in so base a view?
Robbers invade a neighbour's right,
But Love and Justice have more might.
O mean and sordid are the boasts
Of plundered lands and wasted hosts!

Kiugs should by love and justice reign,
Nor be like pirates of the main.
Your clemency to me has shown
A virtue worthy of a throne :
If Heaven has made you great and strong,
Use not her gifts to do us wrong."

　　The lion answered : "It is plain
That I have been abused ; my reign
By slaves and sophisters beset.
But tell me, friend, didst ever yet
Attend in human courts ? You see,
My courtiers say they rule like me."

FABLE II.

THE SPANIEL AND CHAMELEON.

A SPANIEL mightily well bred,
Ne'er taught to labour for his bread,
But to play tricks and bear him smart,
To please his lady's eyes and heart,
Who never had the whip for mischief,
But praises from the damsel—his chief.

　　The wind was soft, the morning fair,
They issued forth to take the air.
He ranged the meadows, where a green
Cameleon—green as grass—was seen.

　　" Halloa ! you chap, who change your coat,
What do you rowing in this boat ?
Why have you left the town ? I say
You're wrong to stroll about this way :

Preferment, which your talent crowns,
Believe me, friend, is found in towns."

"Friend," said the sycophant, "'tis true
One time I lived in town like you.
I was a courtier born and bred,
And kings have bent to me the head.
I knew each lord and lady's passion,
And fostered every vice in fashion.
But Jove was wrath—loves not the liar—
He sent me here to cool my fire,
Retained my nature—but he shaped
My form to suit the thing I aped,
And sent me in this shape obscene,
To batten in a sylvan scene.
How different is your lot and mine!
Lo! how you eat, and drink, and dine;
Whilst I, condemned to thinnest fare,
Like those I flattered, feed on air.
Jove punishes what man rewards;—
Pray you accept my best regards."

FABLE III.

MOTHER, NURSE, AND FAIRY.

"Give me a son, grant me an heir!"
The fairies granted her the prayer.
And to the partial parent's eyes
Was never child so fair and wise;
Waked to the morning's pleasing joy,
The mother rose and sought her boy.

She found the nurse like one possessed,
Who wrung her hands and beat her breast.
"What is the matter, Nurse—this clatter:
The boy is well—what is the matter?"

　"What is the matter? Ah! I fear
The dreadful fairy has been here,
And changed the baby-boy. She came
Invisible; I'm not to blame
She's changed the baby: here's a creature!—
A pug, a monkey, every feature!
Where is his mother's mouth and grace?
His father's eyes, and nose, and face?"

　"Woman," the mother said, "you're blind:
He's wit and beauty all combined."

　"Lord, Madam! with that horrid leer!—
That squint is more than one can bear."

　But, as she spoke, a pigmy wee soul
Jumped in head-foremost through the key-hole,
Perched on the cradle, and from thence
Harangued with fairy vehemence:
　"Repair thy wit—repair thy wit!
Truly, you are devoid of it.
Think you that fairies would change places
With sons of clay and human races—
In one point like to you alone,
That we are partial to our own;
For neither would a fairy mother
Exchange her baby for another;
But should we change with imps of clay,
We should be idiots—like as they."

FABLE IV.

JOVE'S EAGLE, AND MURMURING BEASTS.

As JOVE once on his judgment-seat,
Opened the trap-door at his feet;
Up flew the murmurs of creation,
Of every brute that had sensation.
The Thunderer, therefore, called his Eagle,
Which came obedient as a beagle,—
And him commanded to descend,
And to such murmurs put an end.
The eagle did so—citing all
To answer the imperial call.

   He spoke: "Ye murmurers declare
What are these ills which trouble air?—
Just are the universal laws.
Now let the dog first plead his cause.

   A beagle answered him: "How fleet
The greyhound's course, how nerved his feet!
I hunt by scent, by scent alone;
That lost, and all my chance has flown."

   Answered the greyhound: "If I had
That which he scorns, I should be glad;
Had I the hound's sagacious scent,
I ne'er had murmured discontent."

   The lion murmured he had not
Sly Reynard's wits to lay a plot;
Sly Reynard pleaded that, to awe,
He should possess the lion's paw.
The cock desired the heron's flight;
The heron wished for greater might.

And fish would feed upon the plain,
And beasts would refuge in the main.
None their ambitious wish could smother,
And each was envious of another.
   The eagle answered: "Mutineers,
The god rejects your idle prayers.
But any may exchange who wishes,
And chop and change,—birds, beasts, and fishes."
The eagle paused; but none consented
To quit the race they represented,
And recognised the restless mind
And proud ambition of mankind.

FABLE V.

WILD BOAR AND RAM.

A SHEEP lay tethered, and her life
Fast ebbing on the butcher's knife;
The silly flock looked on with dread.
A wild boar, passing them, then said:
" O cowards! cowards! will nought make
The courage of your hearts awake?
What, with the butcher in your sight,
Flaying—ere life be parted quite—
Your lambs and dams! O stolid race!
Who ever witnessed souls so base?"
   The patriarch ram then answered him:
" My face and bearing are not grim,
But we are not of soul so tame
As to deny Revenge her claim:

We have no whetted tusks to kill,
Yet are not powerless of ill.
Vengeance, the murdering hand pursues,
And retribution claims her dues;
She sends the plagues of war and law,
Where men will battle for a straw—
And our revenge may rest contented,
Since drums and parchment were invented."

—————

FABLE VI.

Miser and Plutus

The wind was high, the window shook,
The miser woke with haggard look;
He stalked along the silent room,
He shivered at the gleam and gloom,
Each lock and every corner eyed,
And then he stood his chest beside;
He opened it, and stood in rapture
In sight of gold he held in capture;
And then, with sudden qualm possessed,
He wrung his hands and beat his breast:
" O, had the earth concealed this gold,
I had perhaps in peace grown old!
But there is neither gold nor price
To recompense the pang of vice.
Bane of all good—delusive cheat,
To lure a soul on to defeat
And banish honour from the mind:
Gold raised the sword midst kith and kind,

Gold fosters each pernicious art
In which the devils bear a part,—
Gold, bane accursed!" In angry mood
Plutus, his god, before him stood.
The trembling miser slammed the chest.
   " What rant and cant have you expressed,
You sordid wretch! It is the mind,
And not the gold, corrupts mankind.
Shall my best medium be accused
Because its virtues are abused?
Virtue and gold alike betrayed,
When knaves demand a cloak to trade;
So likewise power in their possession
Grows into tyrannous oppression.
And in like manner gold may be
Abused to vice and villany.
But when it flows in virtue's streams
It blesses like the sun's blest beams—
Wiping the tears from widowed eyes
And soothing bereft orphans' cries.
Speak not of misers who have sold
Their soul's integrity for gold—
Than bravoes and than cut-throats worse,
Who in their calling steal a purse."

FABLE VII.

LION, FOX, AND GANDER.

A LION, sick of pomp and state,
Resolved his cares to delegate.

Reynard was viceroy named—the crowd
Of courtiers to the regent bowed;
Wolves, bears, and tigers stoop and bend,
And strive who most could condescend;
Whilst he, with wisdom in his face,
Assumed the regal grace and pace.
Whilst flattery hovered him around,
And the pleased ear in thraldom bound,
A fox, well versed in adulation,
Rose to pronounce the due oration:
   " Vast talents, trained in virtue's school,
With clemency, from passion cool—
And uncorrupted—such a hand
Will shed abundance o'er the land.
The brain shall prompt the wiser part,
Mercy and justice rule the heart;
All blessings must attend the nation
Under such bright administration."
   A gander heard and understood,
And summoned round his gosling brood:
" Whene'er you hear a rogue commended,
Be sure some mischief is intended;
A fox now spoke in commendation—
Foxes no doubt will rise in station;
If they hold places, it is plain
The geese will feel a tyrant reign.
'Tis a sad prospect for our race
When every petty clerk in place
Will follow fashion, and ne'er cease
On holidays to feed on geese."

FABLE VIII.

LADY AND WASP.

WHAT stupid nonsense must the Beauty
Endure in her diurnal duty—
Buzzings and whispers from the stores
Of the fatuities of bores!
Yet such impertinence must be pleasing,
Or Beauty would resent such teazing.
A flap will drive a fly away,
A frown will drive a dog to bay:
So if the insects are persistent
'Twas Beauty that was inconsistent!
And if she does not know herself,
Blame not the persecuting elf.

　It chanced upon a summer day
That Doris in her boudoir lay—
She the last work of God's fair creatures,
Contemplated her faultless features.
A wasp assailed her so reclined,
Bred of a persecuting kind.
He now advanced, and now retreated,
Till Beauty's neck and face grew heated;
She smote him with her fan: she said
Wasps were excessively ill bred.
But the wasp answered her: " Alas!
Before you blame me, view your glass.
'Twas beauty caused me to presume;
Those cherry lips, that youthful bloom,
Allured me from the plums and peaches
To Beauty, which the soul o'erreaches."

" Don't hit him, Jenny!" Doris cried :
" The race of wasps is much belied;
I must recant what I have said,—
Wasps are remarkably well bred."
   Away Sir Sting fled, and went boasting
Amongst his fellows—Doris toasting ;
And as his burgundy he sips,
He showed the sugar on his lips.
Away the greedy host then gathered,
Where they thought dalliance fair was feathered.
They fluttered round her, sipped her tea,
And lived in quarters fair and free ;
Nor were they banished, till she found
That wasps had stings and felt the wound.

FABLE IX.

The Bull and the Mastiff.

Deem you to train your son and heir,
For his preceptor then take care ;
To sound his mind your cares employ,
E'er you commit to him your boy.
Once on a time on native plain
A bull enjoyed a native reign.
A mastiff, stranger there, with ire
Beheld the bull, with eyes of fire.
The bovine monarch, on his part,
Spurned up the dust with dauntless heart,
Advised the mastiff to think twice,
And asked—if lust or avarice,

From which, in main, contention springs,
Caused him to break the peace of kings?
The mastiff answered him, 'twas glory—
To emulate the sons of story;
Told him that Cæsar was his sire,
And he a prince baptized in fire;
That rifles and the mitrailleur
Had thrown his bosom in a stir.
  " Accursed cur!" the bull replied,
" Delighting in the sanguine tide:
If you are Revolution trained,
Doubtless your paws with blood are stained—
Demons that take delight in slaughter,
And pour out human blood as water—
Take then thy fate."   With goring wound
The monarch tossed him from the ground
In air gyrating—on the stones
He fell a mass of broken bones.

FABLE X.

ELEPHANT AND BOOKSELLER.

THE traveller whose undaunted soul
Sails o'er the seas from pole to pole
Sees many wonders, which become
So wonderful they strike one dumb,
When we in their description view
Monsters which Adam never knew.
Yet, on the other hand, the sceptic
Supplies his moral antiseptic;

Denying unto truths belief,
With groans which give his ears relief:
But truth is stranger far than fiction,
And outlives sceptic contradiction.
Read Pliny or old Aldrovandus,
If—they would say—you understand us.
Let other monsters stand avaunt,
And read we of the elephant.

   As one of these, in days of yore,
Rummaged a stall of antique lore
Of parchment rolls—not modern binding—
He found a roll; the which unwinding,
He saw all birds and beasts portrayed
Which Nature's bounteous hand had made,
With forms and sentiments, to wit—
All by the hand of man down writ.
The elephant, with great attention,
Remarked upon that great invention:

   " Man is endowed with reason; beasts
Allowed their instinct—that at least:
But here's an author owning neither—
No reason and no instinct either:
He thinks he has all natures known,
And yet he does not know his own.
Now here's the spaniel—who is drawn
The master spirit sprung to fawn.
Pooh, pooh! a courtier in his calling
Must fawn more deeply for enthralling.
Now there's the fox—his attribute
To plunder—as we say, ' to loot.'
Pooh, pooh! a lawyer at that vice
Would outfox Reynard in a trice.

Then come the wolf and tiger's brood;
He bans them for their gust of blood.
Pooh, pooh! he bloodier is than they;
They slay for hunger—he for pay."

A publisher, who heard him speak,
And saw him read Parsee and Greek,
Thought he had found a prize: " Dear sir,
If you against mankind will stir,
And write upon the wrongs of Siam,
No man is better pay than I am;
Or, since 'tis plain that you know true Greek,
To make an onslaught on the rubrick."

Twisting his trunk up like a wipsy,
" Friend," said the elephant, " you're tipsy:
Put up your purse again—be wise;
Leave man mankind to criticise.
Be sure you ne'er will lack a pen
Amidst the bustling sons of men;
For, like to game cocks and such cattle,
Authors run unprovoked to battle,
And never cease to fight and fray them
Whilst there's a publisher to pay them.

FABLE XI.

THE TURKEY, PEACOCK, AND GOOSE.

As specks appear on fields of snow,
So blemishes on beauty show.

A peacock fed in a farm-yard
Where all the poultry eyed him hard—

They looked on him with evil eye,
And mocked his sumptuous pageantry:
Proud of the glories he inherited,
He sought the praises they well merited.
Then, to surprise their dazzled sight,
He spread his glories to the light.
His glories spread, no sooner seen
Than rose their malice and their spleen.
    " Behold his insolence and pride—
His haughtiness!" the turkey cried.
" He trusts in feathers; but within
They serve to hide his negro skin."
    " What hideous legs! " exclaimed the goose;
" The tail to hide them were of use.
And hearken to his voice: it howls
Enough to frighten midnight owls."
    " Yes, they are blemishes, I own,"
Replied the peacock; " harsh the tone
Is of my voice—no symmetry
In my poor legs; yet had your eye
Been pleased to mark my radiant train,
You might have spared detraction's vein.
For if these shanks which you traduce
Belonged to turkey or to goose,
Or had the voice still harsher been,
They had not been remarked or seen;
But Envy, unto beauties blind,
Seeks blemishes to soothe her mind."
    So have we, in the midnight scene,
Seen purity with face serene
Awake the clamour of detraction
From jaundiced Envy's yellow faction.

FABLE XII.

Cupid, Hymen, and Plutus.

As Cupid, with his band of sprites,
In Paphian grove set things to rights,
And trimmed his bow and tipped his arrows,
And taught, to play with Lesbia, sparrows,
Thus Hymen said : " Your blindness makes,
O Cupid, wonderful mistakes !
You send me such ill-coupled folks :
It grieves me, now, to give them yokes.
An old chap, with his troubles laden,
You bind to a light-hearted maiden ;
Or join incongruous minds together,
To squabble for a pin or feather
Until they sue for a divorce ;
To which the wife assents—of course."

  " It is your fault, and none of mine,"
Cupid replied. " I hearts combine :
You trade in settlements and deeds,
And care not for the heart that bleeds.
You couple them for gold and fee ;
Complain of Plutus—not of me."

  Then Plutus added : " What can I do ?—
The settlement is what they spy to.
Say, does Belinda blame her fate ?—
She only asked a great estate.
Doris was rich enough, but humble :
She got a title—does she grumble ?
All men want money—not a shoe-tie
Care they for excellence or beauty.

Oh all, my boys, is right enough:
They get the money—hearts is stuff."

FABLE XIII.

THE TAMED FAWN.

A YOUNG stag in the brake was caught,
And home with corded antlers brought.
The lord was pleased: so was the clown
When he was tipped with half-a-crown.
The stag was dragged before his wife;
The gentle lady begged its life:
" How sleek its skin! how specked like ermine!
Sure never creature was more charming."
    At first within the court confined,
He fled and hid from all mankind;
Then, bolder grown, with mute amaze
He at safe distance stood to gaze;
Then munched the linen on the lines,
And off a hood or whimple dines;
Then steals my little master's bread,
Then followed servants to be fed,
Then poked his nose in fists for meat,
And though repulsed would not retreat;
Thrusts at them with his levelled horns,
And man, that was his terror, scorns.
    How like unto the country maid,
Who of a red-coat, first, afraid
Will hide behind the door, to trace
The magic of the martial lace;

But soon before the door will stand,
Return the jest and strike the hand;
Then hangs with pride upon his arm,—
For gallant soldiers bear a charm,—
Then seeks to spread her conquering fame,
For custom conquers fear and shame.

FABLE XIV.

THE MONKEY WHO HAD SEEN THE WORLD.

A monkey, to reform the times,
Resolved to visit foreign climes;
For therefore toilsomely we roam
To bring politer manners home.
Misfortunes serve to make us wise:
Poor pug was caught, and made a prize;
Sold was he, and by happy doom
Bought to cheer up a lady's gloom.
Proud as a lover of his chains
His way he wins, his post maintains—
He twirled her knots and cracked her fan,
Like any other gentleman.
When jests grew dull he showed his wit,
And many a lounger hit with it.
When he had fully stored his mind—
As Orpheus once for human kind,—
So he away would homewards steal,
To civilize the monkey weal.
 The hirsute sylvans round him pressed,
Astonished to behold him dressed.

They praise his sleeve and coat, and hail
His dapper periwig and tail;
His powdered back, like snow, admired,
And all his shoulder-knot desired.
　" Now mark and learn : from foreign skies
I come, to make a people wise.
Weigh your own worth, assert your place,—
The next in rank to human race.
In cities long I passed my days,
Conversed with man and learnt his ways;
Their dress and courtly manners see—
Reform your state and be like me.
　" Ye who to thrive in flattery deal,
Must learn your passions to conceal;
And likewise to regard your friends
As creatures sent to serve your ends.
Be prompt to lie : there is no wit
In telling truth, to lose by it.
And knock down worth, bespatter merit :
Don't stint—all will your scandal credit.
Be bumptious, bully, swear, and fight—
And all will own the man polite."
　He grinned and bowed.　With muttering jaws
His pugnosed brothers grinned applause,
And, fond to copy human ways,
Practise new mischiefs all their days.
　　Thus the dull lad too big to rule,
　With travel finishes his school;
　Soars to the heights of foreign vices,
　And copies—reckless what their price is.

FABLE XV.

PHILOSOPHER AND PHEASANT.

A sage awakened by the dawn,
By music of the groves was drawn
From tree to tree: responsive notes
Arose from many warbling throats.
As he advanced, the warblers ceased;
Silent the bird and scared the beast—
The nightingale then ceased her lay,
And the scared leveret ran away.
The sage then pondered, and his eye
Roamed round to learn the reason why.

He marked a pheasant, as she stood
Upon a bank, above her brood;
With pride maternal beat her breast
As she harangued and led from nest:
"Play on, my infant brood—this glen
Is free from bad marauding men.
O trust the hawk, and trust the kite,
Sooner than man—detested wight!
Ingratitude sticks to his mind,—
A vice inherent to the kind.
The sheep, that clothes him with her wool,
Dies at the shambles—butcher's school;
The honey-bees with waxen combs
Are slain by hives and hecatombs;
And the sagacious goose, who gives
The plume whereby he writes and lives,
And as a guerdon for its use
He cuts the quill and eats the goose.

Avoid the monster : where he roams
He desolates our raided homes ;
And where such acts and deeds are boasted,
I hear we pheasants all are roasted."

FABLE XVI.

Pin and Needle.

A PIN which long had done its duty,
Attendant on a reigning beauty,—
Had held her muffler, fixed her hair,
And made its mistress *debonnaire*,—
Now near her heart in honour placed,
Now banished to the rear disgraced ;
From whence, as partners of her shame,
She saw the lovers served the same.
From whence, thro' various turns of life,
She saw its comforts and its strife :
With tailors warm, with beggars cold,
Or clutched within a miser's hold.
His maxim racked her wearied ear :
" A pin a day 's a groat a year."
Restored to freedom by the proctor,
She paid some visits with a doctor ;
She pinned a bandage that was crossed,
And thence, at Gresham Hall, was lost.
Charmed with its wonders, she admires,
And now of this, now that inquires—
'Twas plain, in noticing her mind,
She was of virtuoso kind.

" What's this thing in this box, dear sir?"
" A needle," said the interpreter.
" A needle shut up in a box?
Good gracious me, why sure it locks!
And why is it beside that flint?
I could give her now a good hint:
If she were handed to a sempstress,
She would hem more and she would clem less."
" Pin!" said the needle, " cease to blunder:
Stupid alike your hints and wonder.
This is a loadstone, and its virtue—
Though insufficient to convert you—
Makes me a magnet; and afar
True am I to my polar star.
The pilot leaves the doubtful skies,
And trusts to me with watchful eyes;
By me the distant world is known,
And both the Indies made our own.
I am the friend and guide of sailors,
And you of sempstresses and tailors."

FABLE XVII.

SHEPHERD'S DOG AND WOLF.

A HUNGRY wolf had thinned the fold,
Safely he refuged on the wold;
And, as in den secure he lay,
The thefts of night regaled his day.
The shepherd's dog, who searched the glen,
By chance found the marauder's den.

They fought like Trojan and like Greek,
Till it fell out they both waxed weak.
 "Wolf," said the dog, " the whilst we rest on,
I fain would ask of you a question."
 " Ask on," the wolf replied; " I'm ready."
 "Wolf," said the dog, " with soul so steady
And limbs so strong, I wonder much
That you our lambs and ewes should touch.
There are the lion and the boar
To bathe your jaws with worthier gore;
'Tis cowardly to raid the fold."
 " Friend," said the wolf, " I pray thee, hold!
Nature framed me a beast of prey,
And I must eat when, where I may.
Now if your bosom burn with zeal
To help and aid the bleating-weal,
Hence to your lord and master : say
What you have said to me; or, stay,
Tell him that I snatch, now and then,
One sheep for thousands gorged by men.
I am their foe, and called a curse,
But a pretended friend is worse."

FABLE XVIII.

The Unsatisfactory Painter.

Lest captious men suspect your story,
Speak modestly its history.
The traveller, who overleaps the bounds
Of probability, confounds;

But though men hear your deeds with phlegm,
You may with flattery cram them.
Hyperboles, though ne'er so great,
Will yet come short of self-conceit.
  A painter drew his portraits truly,
And marked complexion and mien duly;—
Really a fellow knew the picture,
There was nor flattery nor delicture.
The eyes, and mouth, and faulty nose,
Were all showed up in grim repose;
He marked the dates of youth and age—
But so he lost his clientage:
The which determined to recover,
He turned in mind the matter over.
He bought a pair of busts—one, Venus,
The other was Apollo Phœbus;
Above his subject client placed them,
And for the faulty features traced them.
Chatted the while of Titian's tints,
Of Guido—Raphael—neither stints
To raise him to the empyrëal,
Whilst he is sketching his ideal.
He sketches, utters, "That will do:
Be pleased, my lord, to come and view."
" I thought my mouth a little wider."
" My lord, my lord, you me deride, ah! "
" Such *was* my nose when I was young."
" My lord, you have a witty tongue."
" Ah well, ah well! you artists flatter."
" That were, my lord, no easy matter."
" Ah well, ah well! you artists see best."
" My lord, I only (*aside*) earn my fee best."

So with a lady—he, between us,
Borrowed the face and form of Venus.
There was no fear of its rejection—
Her lover voted it perfection.
So on he went to fame and glory,
And raised his price—which ends the story;—
But not the moral,—which, though fainter,
Bids one to scorn an honest painter.

FABLE XIX.

Lion and Cub.

All men are fond of rule and place,
Though granted by the mean and base;
Yet all superior merit fly,
Nor will endure an equal nigh.
They o'er some ale-house club preside
With smoke and joke and paltry pride.
Nay, e'en with blockheads pass the night;
If such can read, to such I write.
  A lion cub of sordid mind
Avoided all the lion-kind,
And, greedy of applause, sought feasts
With asses and ignoble beasts;
There, as their president appears,
An ass in every point, but ears.
If he would perpetrate a joke,
They brayed applause before he spoke;
And when he spoke, with shout they praised,
And said he beautifully brayed.

Elate with adulation, then
He sought his father's royal den,
And brayed a bray. The lion started,
The noble heart within him smarted.
" You lion cub," he said, " your bray
Proclaims where you pass night and day,—
'Midst coxcombs who, with shameless face,
Blush not proclaiming their disgrace."

" Father, the club deems very fine,
All that conforms with asinine."

" My son, what stupid asses prize
Lions and nobler brutes despise."

FABLE XX.

OLD HEN AND YOUNG COCK.

ONCE an old hen led forth her brood
To scratch and glean and peck for food;
A chick, to give her wings a spell,
Fluttered and tumbled in a well.
The mother wept till day was done,
When she met with a grown-up son,
And thus addressed him:—" My dear boy,
Your years and vigour give me joy:
You thrash all cocks around, I'm told;
'Tis right, cocks should be brave and bold:
But never—fears I cannot quell—
Never, my son, go near that well;
A hateful, false, and wretched place,
Which is most fatal to my race.

Imprint that counsel on your breast,
And trust to providence the rest."
He thanked the dame's maternal care,
And promised never to go near.
Yet still he burned to disobey,
And hovered round it day by day;
And communed thus : " I wonder why?
Does mother think my soul is shy?
Thinks me a coward? or does she
Store grain in yonder well from me?
I'll find that out, and so here goes."
So said, he flaps his wings and crows,
Mounted the margin, peered below,
Where to repel him rose a foe.
His choler rose, his plumes upreared—
With ruffled plumes the foe appeared.
Challenged to fight—he dashed him down
Upon the mirrored wave to drown;
And drowning uttered : " This condition
Comes from my mother's prohibition.
Did she forget, or not believe,
That I too am a son of Eve ? "

FABLE XXI.

The Ratcatcher and Cats.

The rats by night the mischief did,
And Betty every morn was chid.
The cheese was nibbled, tarts were taken,
And purloined were the eggs and bacon;

And Betty cursed the cat, whose duty
Was to protect and guard the booty.
A ratcatcher, of well known skill,
Was called to kill or scotch the ill;
And, as an engineer, surveyed
Their haunts and laid an ambuscade.
A cat beheld him, and was wrath,
Whilst she resolved to cross his path;
Not to be beaten by such chaps,
She silently removed his traps.
Again he set the traps and toils,
Again his cunning pussy foils.
He set a trap to catch the thief,
And pussy she got caught in brief.
" Ah!" said the rat-catcher, " you scamp,
You are the spy within the camp."
But the cat said, " A sister spare,
Your science is our mutual care."
" Science and cats!" the man replied;
" We soon that question shall decide;
You are my rival interloper,
A nasty, sneaking, crouching groper."
  A sister tabby saw the cord,
And interposed a happy word:
" In every age and clime we see
Two of a trade cannot agree;
Each deems the other an encroacher,
As sportsman thinks another poacher.
Beauty with beauty vies in charms,
And king with king in warfare's arms:
But let us limit our desires,
Nor war like beauties, kings, and squires;

For though one prey we both pursue
There's prey enough for us and you."

FABLE XXII.

THE SHAVEN AND SHORN GOAT.

'Tis strange to see a new-launched fashion
Lay on the soul and grow a passion.
To illustrate such folly, I
Proffer some beast to the mind's eye.
Now I select the goat.   What then?
I never said goats equal men.
  A goat of singularity—
Not vainer than a goat need be—
Lay on a thymy bank, and viewed
Himself reflected in the flood.
" Confound my beard ! " he thought, and said ;
" How badly it becomes my head ;
Upon my honour ! women might
Take me to be some crazy wight."
He sought the barber of the place,—
A monkey 'twas, of Moorish race,
Who shaved mankind, drew teeth, and bled.
A pole diagonal—striped red,
Teeth in their row in order strung,
And pewter bason by them slung,
Far in the street projecting stood—
The pole with bandage symboled blood.
  Pug shaved our friend and took his penny,
And hoped to shave him oft and many :

D

Goatee, impatient of applause,
Then sought his native hills and shaws.
" Heigh-day ! how now ? whoever heard—
What gone and shaven off your beard ? "
    The fop replied : " All realms polite,
From Roman to the Muscovite,
Now trim their beards and shave their chins ;
Shall we, like Monkish Capuchins,
Alone be singular and hairy ?
One walks amidst the cities cheery,
And men and boys all cease to poke
Fun at the beard by way of joke—
In days of old, so Romans jeered
Stoic philosophers with beard."
    " Friend," said a bearded chieftain, " you
At Rome may do as Romans do ;
But if you refuge with our herd,
I counsel you to keep your beard :
For if you dread the jeers of others,
How will you bear it from your brothers ? "

FABLE XXIII.

OLD DAME AND CATS.

HE who holds friendship with a knave,
Will reputation hardly save ;
And thus upon our choice of friends
Our good or evil name depends.
    A wrinkled hag—of naughty fame—
Sat hovering o'er a flickering flame,

Propped with both hands upon her knees
She shook with palsy and the breeze.
She had perhaps seen fourscore years,
And backwards said her daily prayers;
Her troop of cats with hunger mewed,—
Tabbies and toms, a numerous brood.
Teased with their murmuring, out she flew
In angry passion : " Hence, ye crew !—
What made me take to keeping cats?
Ye are as bad as bawling brats :
With brats I might perhaps have grown rich ;
I never had been thought a known witch.
Boys pester me, and strive to awe—
Across my path they place a straw;
They nail the horse-shoe, hide the broom-stick,
Put pins, and every sort of trick."
  " Dame," said a tabby, " cease your prate,
Enough to break a pussy's pate.
What is our lot beneath your roof?
Within, starvation ; out, reproof :
Elsewhere we had been honest mousers,
And slept, by, fireside carousers.
Here we are imps who serve a hag,
And yonder broom-stick's thought your nag ;
Boys hunt us with a doom condign,
To take one life out of our nine."

FABLE XXIV.

Butterfly and Snail.

All upstarts, insolent in place,
Remind us of their vulgar race.

    A butterfly, but born one morning,
Sat on a rose, the rosebud scorning.
His wings of azure, jet, and gold,
Were truly glorious to behold;
He spread his wings, he sipped the dew,
When an old neighbour hove in view—
The snail, who left a slimy trace
Upon the lawn, his native place.

    " Adam," he to the gard'ner cried,
" Behold this fellow by my side;
What is the use with daily toil
To war with weeds, to clear the soil,
And with keen intermittent labour
To graft and prune for fruit with flavour
The peach and plum, if such as he,
Voracious vermin, may make free?
Give them the roller or the rake,
And crush as you would crush a snake."

    The snail replied: " Your arrogance
Awakes my patience from its trance;
Recalls to mind your humble birth,
Born from the lowliest thing on earth.
Nine times has Phœbus, with the hours,
Awakened to new life, new flowers,
Since you were a vile crawling thing!
Though now endowed with painted wing,

You then were vilest of the vile—
I was a snail, but housed the while;
Was born a snail, and snail shall die;
And thou, though now a butterfly,
Will leave behind a baneful breed
Of caterpillar sons—thy seed."

<hr/>

FABLE XXV.

The Scold and Parrot.

A HUSBAND said unto his wife:
" Who deals in slander deals in strife;
Are we the heralds of disgrace,
To thunder, love, at all our race—
And, indiscriminate in rage,
To spare nor friend nor sex nor age?
Your tongue, love, is a rolling flood
That thundering onwards stirs up mud,
And, like to fame and human woes,
Progressing, strengthens as it flows."

  "My husband," so the *tongue* replies,
" So philosophic and so wise,
Am I to be—so wisdom ridden—
A parrot's privilege forbidden?
You praise his talk—smile at his squalling
Yet in your wife you deem it brawling:
Dear husband, must it still belong
To man to think his wife is wrong?
A lesson learnt from nature's school
Tells me to call a fool a fool."

But Nature disabused her words
By cat and monkey, dog and birds :
Puss spat and pug grinned at the scold,
The hound slunk off, the magpie told,
With repetitions, woman's rage ;
Whilst poll, haranguing from her cage :
" Parrots for prattling words are prized ;
Woman for prattling words despised.
She who attacks another's fame
Does but discredit her own name ;
Upon her tongues malignant set,
And with good interest pay their debt."

FABLE XXVI.

Cur and Mastiff.

A SNEAKING cur caused much disaster
By pandering scandal for his master.
The hound was beaten, mastiff chidden,
Puss in disgrace, and pug forbidden.
Each of his dearest chum grew shy,
And none could tell a reason why.
Burglars to rob the house laid wait.
Betty in love, undid the gate ;
The cur was won by dint of meat ;
Remained the mastiff dog to cheat.
The mastiff dog refused the bribe,
And tore the hand of one beside.
The cur off with the tidings ran,
And told how he had bit a man.

The master said: "Hanged he shall be!"
They dragged poor Trusty to the tree:
He met his master, and averred
That he had been condemned unheard.
   His lord then sat to hear the trial:
The mastiff pleaded his denial;
The cur then, special pleading, stated
The case—unduly aggravated.
   When evidence on either side
Concluded was, the dog replied,
And ended with this peroration:
" Trust not to curs of basest station,
With itching palms—a plot is laid,
And man and master are betrayed."
   The mastiff had with truth harangued:
The truth appeared; the cur was hanged.

FABLE XXVII.

Sick Man and Angel.

" Is there no hope?" the sick man said.
The silent doctor shook his head,
And took his leave with unfeigned sorrow
To lose a patient on the morrow.
When left alone, the dying man
" Let me review my life"—began;
" My bargains—well, they were well made;
'Tis the necessity of trade—
Necessity is no transgression.
Now for my portion in possession:

My lands and my securities,
They all are right, in every wise.
If justice to myself and heirs
Have done some hardships unawares,—
Left Smith in jail for debt, or sent
The Browns adrift for unpaid rent,—
I've given alms and helped my friends,
What I propose will make amends:
When I am numbered with the dead,
And when my good bequests are read,
Then will be seen and then be known
Benevolence I have not shown."

   The angel, present by his side,
Bade him not in such hopes confide:

   " What deed have you done worthy praise?
What orphan blesses, widow prays,
To lengthen out your life one year?
If you will now add deeds to prayer—
Your neighbours want, whilst you abound—
Give me a cheque—five hundred pound."

   " Where is the haste?" the sick man whines;
" Who knows—who knows what Heaven designs:
That sum, and more, are in my will;
Perhaps I may recover still."

   " Fool!" said the angel: " it is plain
That your great happiness was gain;
And after death would fain atone
By giving what is not your own."
" Whilst there is life, there's hope!" he cried;
" Then why such haste?"—he spoke, and died.

FABLE XXVIII.

THE PERSIAN, THE SUN, AND THE CLOUD.

LIVES there a bard for genius famed
Whom Envy's tongue hath not declaimed?
Her hissing snakes proclaim her spite;
She summons up the fiends of night;
Hatred and malice by her stand,
And prompt to do what she command.

   As prostrate to the orb of day
A Persian, invocating, lay:
   " Parent of light, whose rays dispense
The various gifts of Providence,
Accept our praise, accept our prayer,
Smile on our fields, and bless our year."

   A cloud passed by—a voice aloud,
Like Envy's, issued from that cloud:
   " I can eclipse your gaudy orb,
And every ray you ask absorb.
Pray, then, to me—where praise is due—
And I will grant the rays to you."

   The Persian answered in his wrath:
" He raised thee to that airy path;
A passing wind or puff of air
Will hurl thee to thy proper sphere."

   The gale arose, the cloud was doomed,
The golden orb his reign resumed.
And as the sun above, so worth
Scatters the clouds of sons of earth.

FABLE XXIX.

THE DYING FOX.

A FOX was dying, and he lay
In all the weakness of decay.
A numerous progeny, with groans,
Attended to his feeble tones:
  "My crimes lie heavy on my soul;
My sons, my sons, your raids control!
Ah, how the shrieks of murdered fowl
Environ me with stunning howl!"
  The hungry foxes in a ring
Looked round, but saw there no such thing:
"This is an ecstasy of brain:
We fast, dear sir, and wish in vain."
  "Gluttons! restrain such wish," replied
The dying fox; "be such defied;
Inordinate desires deplore;
The more you win, you grieve the more.
Do not the dogs betray our pace,
And gins and guns destroy our race?
Old age—which few of us attain—
Now puts a period to my pain.
Would you the good name lost redeem?
Live, then, in credit and esteem."
  "Good counsel, marry!" said a fox;
"And quit our mountain-dens and rocks!
But if we quit our native place,
We bear the name that marks our race;
And what our ancestry have done
Descends to us from sire to son.

Though we should feed like harmless lambs,
We should regarded be as shams;
The change would never be believed;
A name lost cannot be retrieved."

The Sire replied: "Too true; but then—
Hark! that's the cackle of a hen.
Go, but be moderate, spare the brood:
One chicken, one, might do me good."

FABLE XXX.

THE SETTER AND THE PARTRIDGE.

THE setting dog the stubble tried,
And snuffed the breeze with nostrils wide;
He set—the sportsmen from behind,
Conscious of game, the net unwind.

A partridge, which as warder stood,
Warned, and the covey sought the wood.
But, ere she followed from her cover,
Thus she discharged her mind on Rover:

"Thou fawning slave and sneaking cheat,
Subservient unto man's deceit!
Disgrace unto thy honest race,
Unto the race of dogs disgrace;
Who ere to men they bent the knee
Were noted for fidelity."

The dog retorted with a sneer:
"Since you are safe, enjoy your jeer;
Rustic alike in kind and mind,
And ignorant of courts refined.

Sagacious courtiers do like me,—
They rise to high supremacy;
I copy them, and I inherit
The high rewards for worth and merit."
  "I might have known," the partridge said.
"The school where you were trained and bred;
With a smooth brow for every crisis,
Inherent to your master's vices.
You came from courts : return! adieu"—
And to her covey off she flew.

FABLE XXXI.

The Universal Apparition.

A RAKE who had, by pleasure stuffing,
Raked mind and body down to nothing,
In wretched vacancy reclined,
Enfeebled both in frame and mind.
  As pain and languor chose to bore him,
A ghastly phantom rose before him :
  "My name is Care. Nor wealth nor power
Can give the heart a cheerful hour
Devoid of health—impressed by care.
From pleasures fraught with pains, forbear."
  The phantom fled. The rake abstained,
And part of fleeing health retained.
Then, to reform, he took a wife,
Resolved to live a sober life.
  Again the phantom stood before him,
With jealousies and fears to bore him.

Her smiles to others he resents,
Looks to the charges and the rents,
Increasing debts, perplexing duns,
And nothing for the younger sons.

He turned his thoughts to lucre's thirst,
And stored until his garners burst:
The spectre haunted him the more.
Then poverty besieged his door:
He feared the burglar and the thief;
Nor light nor darkness brought relief.

Therefore he turned his thoughts to power,
To guard him in the midnight hour.
That he achieved—and then the sprite
Beleagued him morning, noon, and night.
He had no placid hour for rest;
Envy and hate his soul depressed,
And rivalry, and foe for friend,
And footfalls which his steps attend.

Therefore he sought a rustic bower—
Groves, fields, and fruit-trees, filled each hour;
But droughts and rains, and blighting dews,
On foot, on horseback, Care pursues.

He faced the phantom, and addressed:
" Since you must ever be my guest,
Let me, as host, perform my due;
Go you the first, I'll follow you."

FABLE XXXII.

The Owls and Sparrow.

Two pompous owls together sat
In the solemnity of chat :
  " Respect to wisdom, all is fled ;
The Grecian sages all are dead.
They gave our fathers honour due ;
The dignity of owls they knew.
Upon our merit they conferred
The title of 'The Athenian bird.' "

  " Brother, they did ; you reason right,"
Answered his chum with winking sight.
" For Athens was the seat of learning.
Academicians *were* discerning.
They placed us on Minerva's helm,
And strove with rank to overwhelm
Our worth, which now is quite neglected,—
Ay, a cock-sparrow 's more respected."

  A sparrow who was passing by,
And heard the speech, made this reply :
" Old chaps, you were at Athens graced,
And on Minerva's helm were placed,
And we all know the reason why.
Of all the birds beneath the sky,
They chose you forth the lot to show
What they desired their schools to know,
The emptiness of solemn looks.
You teach it better than the books.
Would you be thought of wit and worth,
And be respected upon earth,

Humble your arrogance of mind,
Go to the farmers, and there find
A welcome—foe to mice and rats.
And live the rivals of the cats."

FABLE XXXIII.

COURTIER AND PROTEUS.

THE country shelters the disgrace
Of every courtier out of place:
When, doomed to exercise and health,
O'er his estate he scatters wealth;
There he builds schemes for others' ruin,
As Philip's son of old was doing.
    A wandless one, upon the strand,
Wandered with heavy hours on hand:
The murmuring waters ran and broke;
Proteus arose, and him bespoke:
    " Come ye from court, I ask? Your mien
Is so importantly serene."
    The courtier answered, friends had tricked him,
And that he was a party's victim.
    Proteus replied: " I hold the skill
To change to any shape at will.
But I am told at court there be
Fellows who more than rival me.
Now see a form that I can take:"
And Proteus rolled a scaly snake.
    The man replied: " Of reptile race
Is every courtier, whilst in place.

Yes, they can take the dragon form,
Bask in the sun, and flee the storm;
With envy glare, with malice gloat,
And cast, like you your skin,—their coat!
And in a dunghill born and bred,
With new-born lustre rear the head."

    Then Proteus as a lion stood,
And shook his mane and stirred the flood;
Then soused as waters, soared as fire,
Then as a tigress glared with ire.

    " Such transformations might appal,
Had I not stood in regal hall.
We hunt the lion, utilise
The elements, without surprise.
Such forms indeed are things of prey,
And courtiers hunt them, though they bray.
They practise frauds in every shape,
Or as a lion or an ape."

    So said, the courtier grasped the god,
Bound him with cords, dragged to the sod,
And said: " Now tell me, Proteus; tell,
Do men or ancient gods excel?
For you are bound to tell the truth,
Nor are your transformations sooth;
But courtiers are not bound by ties;
They consort not with truth, but lies;
Fix on him any form you will
A courtier finds evasion still."

FABLE XXXIV.

The Mastiff.

Those who in quarrels interpose
Must often wipe a bloody nose.

A mastiff of true English mood
Loved fighting better than his food.
When dogs were snarling o'er a bone
He wished to make their war his own ;
And often found (where two contend)
To interpose, obtained his end :
The scars of honour seamed his face ;
He deemed his limp endued with grace.

Once on a time he heard afar
Two dogs contend with noisy jar ;
Away he scoured to lay about him,
Resolved no fray should be without him.
Forth from the yard—which was a tanner's—
The master rushed to teach him manners ;
And with the cudgel tanned his hide,
And bullied him with words beside.
Forth from another yard—a butcher's—
The master rushed—his name was Mutchers—
" Why, who the deuce are you ? " he cried :
" Why do you interfere ? Bankside
Has, at the Bull-pit, seen and known,
And Hockleyhole and Marry-bone,
That when we go to work we mean it—
Why should you come and intervene it ? "
So said, they dragged the dogs asunder,
And kicks and clubs fell down like thunder.

E

And parted now, and freed from danger,
The curs beheld the meddling stranger,
And where their masters whacked they hurried,
And master mastiff he was " worried."

FABLE XXXV.

BARLEYMOW AND DUNGHILL.

How many saucy beaux we meet
'Twixt Westminster and Aldgate-street !
Rascals—the mushrooms of a day,
Who sprung and shared the South Sea prey,
Nor in their zenith condescend
To own or know the humble friend.
  A careful farmer took his way
Across his yard at break of day :
He leant a moment o'er the rail,
To hear the music of the flail ;
In his quick eye he viewed his stock,—
The geese, the hogs, the fleecy flock.
  A barleymow there, fat as mutton,
Then held her master by the button :
" Master, my heart and soul are wrung—till
They can't abide that dirty dunghill :
Master, you know I make your beer—
You boast of me at Christmas cheer ;
Then why insult me and disgrace me,
And next to that vile dunghill place me ?
By Jove ! it gives my nose offence :
Command the hinds to cart it hence."

" You stupid Barleymow," said Dunghill ;
" You talk about your heart and wrung-ill :
Where would you be, I'd like to know,
Had I not fed and made you grow ?
You of October brew brag—pshaw !
You would have been a husk of straw.
And now, instead of gratitude,
You rail in this ungrateful mood."

FABLE XXXVI.

PYTHAGORAS AND COUNTRYMAN.

PYTHAGORAS, at daybreak drawn
To meditate on dewy lawn,
To breathe the fragrance of the morning,
And, like philosophers, all scorning
To think or care where he was bound,
Fell on a farm. A hammer's sound
Arrested then his thoughts and ear:
   " My man, what are you doing there ? "
   The clown stood on a ladder's rung,
And answered him with rudish tongue :
" I've caught the villain—this here kite
Kept my hens ever in a fright;
I've nailed he here to my barn-door,
Him shan't steal turkey-pouts no more."
And lo ! upon the door displayed,
The caitiff kite his forfeit paid.
   " Friend," said Pythagoras, " 'tis right
To murder a marauding kite ;

But, by analogy, that glutton—
That man who feasts on beef and mutton—
I say,—that by analogy,—
The man who eats a chick should die.
'Tis insolence of power and might
When man, the glutton, kills the kite."

 The clown, who heard Pythagoras,
Waxed in a rage, called him an ass;
Said man was lord of all creation.

 " Man," the sage answered, *sans* sensation,
" You murder hawks and kites, lest they
Should rob you of your fatted prey;
And that great rogues may hold their state,
The petty rascal meets his fate."

FABLE XXXVII.

Farmer's Wife and Raven.

" Why are those tears? Why droops your head?
Say is your swain or husband dead?" .

 The farmer's wife said: " You know well
The salt was spilt,—to me it fell;
And then to add loss unto loss,
The knife and fork were laid across.
On Friday evening, 'tis too true,
Bounce in my lap a coffin flew.
Some dire misfortune it portends:
I tremble for my absent friends."

 " Dame," said the neighbour, " tremble not:
Be all these prodigies forgot;

The while, at least, you eat your dinner
Bid the foul fiend avaunt—the sinner!
And soon as Betty clears the table
For a dessert, I'll read a fable.
  " Betwixt her panniers rocked, on Dobbin
A matron rode to market bobbing,
Indulging in a trancelike dream
Of money for her eggs and cream;
When direful clamour from her broke:
' A raven on the left-hand oak!
His horrid croak bodes me some ill.'
Here Dobbin stumbled; 'twas down-hill,
And somehow he with failing legs
Fell, and down fell the cream and eggs.
She, sprawling, said, ' You rascal craven!
You – nasty—filthy—dirty—raven!'
' Goody,' said raven, ' spare your clamour,
There nothing here was done by glamour;
Get up again and wipe your gown,
It was not I who threw you down;
For had you laid your market ware
On Dun—the old sure-footed mare—
Though all the ravens in the Hundred
Had croaked till all the Hundred wondered,
Sure-footed Dun had kept her legs,
And you, good woman, saved your eggs.' "

FABLE XXXVIII.

The Turkey and the Ant.

We blame the mote that dims the eye
Of other men, whose faults we spy;
But we ignore the beam that lies
With stronger strain in one's own eyes.
   A turkey, who grew dull at home,
Resolved in the wild woods to roam;
Wearied she was of barn-door food,
Therefore she chuckled round her brood,
And said, " My little ones, now follow;
We'll go and dine in yonder hollow."
They first upon an ant-hill fell—
Myriads of negro-ants, pell-mell—
" O gobble, gobble—here's a treat!
Emmets are most delicious meat;
Spare not, spare not. How blest were we,
Could we here live from poulterers free!
Accursèd man on turkeys preys,
Christmas to us no holy-days;
When with the oyster-sauce and chine
We roast that aldermen may dine.
They call us 'alderman in chains,'
With sausages—the stupid swains!
Ah! gluttony is sure the first
Of all the seven sins—the worst!
I'd choke mankind, had I the power,
From peasant's hut to lordly bower."
   An ant, who on a neighbouring beech
Had climbed the trunk beyond her reach,

Thus said to her : " You turkey-hen,
What right have you to rail on men ?
You nor compunction know nor feel,
But gobble nations at a meal ! "

FABLE XXXIX.

THE FATHER AND JUPITER.

A MAN to Jupiter preferred
Prayers for a wife : his prayer was heard.
Jove smiled to see the man caressing
The granted prayer and doubtful blessing.
　Again he troubled Jove with prayers :
Fraught with a wife, he wanted heirs :
They came, to be annoys or joys—
One girl and two big bouncing boys.
And, a third time, he prayed his prayer
For grace unto his son and heir—
That he, who should his name inherit,
Might be replete with worth and merit.
Then begged his second might aspire,
With strong ambition, martial fire ;
That Fortune he might break or bend,
And on her neck to heights ascend.
Last, for the daughter, prayed that graces
Might tend upon her face and paces.
　Jove granted all and every prayer,
For daughter, and cadet, and heir.
The heir turned out a thorough miser,
And lived as lives the college sizar ;

He took no joy in show or feat,
And starving did not choose to eat.
The soldier—he held honours martial,
And won the baton of field-marshal;
And then, for a more princely elf,
They laid the warrior on the shelf.
The beauty viewed with high disdain
The lover's hopes—the lover's pain;
Age overtook her, undecided,
And Cupid left her much derided.

    The father raised his voice above,
Complaining of the gifts to Jove;
But Jove replied that weal and woe
Depended not on outward show—
That ignorant of good or ill,
Men still beset the heavenly will:
The blest were those of virtuous mind,
Who were to Providence resigned.

FABLE XL.

The Two Monkeys.

The scholar, of his learning vain,
Beholds the fop with deep disdain:
The fop, with spirit as discerning,
Looks down upon the man of learning.
The Spanish Don—a solemn strutter—
Despises Gallic airs and flutter:
Whilst the Gaul ridicules the Don,
As one to poke his fun upon;

And John Bull looks with like disdain
On manners both of France and Spain :
They hold, indeed, a deed tripartite
To see each other in a tart light.
'Tis thus the bard is scorned by those
Who only deal in learned prose :
Whilst bards of quick imagination
Are hipped by the dull prose oration.
Men scoff at apes : apes scoff at them ;
And all—except themselves—contemn.

   Two monkeys visited the fair,
Like critics, with Parnassian sneer ;
They forced a way through draggled folk,
Laughed at Jack Pudding and his joke,
Then bought their tickets for the show,
And squatted in the foremost row ;
Their cut-of-jib was there so stunning,
It set the idle rabble funning.

   " Brother," one Pug to other said,
" The mob is certainly ill-bred."
A sentiment which found no favour,
And the retorts were of ill-savour.

   The clown with entrance stopped the jar—
Head over heels—with " Here we are ! "
The tumblers made their somersets,
The vaulters made tremendous jets ;
The dancer on the rope did wonders,
And drew down the applauses—thunders,
As Numa once elicited
From Jove Elicius, so they did.

   " Behold the imitative crew ! "
Said Pug : " they copy me and you,

And clumsily. I'd like to see
Them jump from forest-tree to tree;
I'd like to see them, on a twig,
Perform a slip-slap or a rig;
And yet it pleasant is to know
The boobies' estimate us so."
  "Brother!" the other Pug replied,
" They do their best—with us their guide;
We must allow praise is their due,
Whilst they example good pursue;
But when I see them take a flight,
Or walk, like they walk—bolt upright,
Because we sometimes walk on two—
I hate the imitative crew!"

FABLE XLI.

Owl and Farmer.

An owl took, in a barn, a station
As fittest for deep contemplation;
There (like a Turk) upon a beam
He sat, as Turks sit in hareem.
  So smokers, at the Magpie met,
Peruse the ' Post-boy ' or ' Gazette;'
And thence foretell, in wise and sure hope,
The future destinies of Europe.
  The farmer comes to see his sheaves.
The owl his silent soul relieves;
" Reason in man is sheer pretence,
Would he—were he endowed with sense—

Treat owls with scorning ? He can praise
The birds that twitter on the sprays :
Linnets, and larks, and nightingales,
Yet in the nobler owl he fails.
Should I, by daylight, view my reign,
Those birds would cluster in my train ;
Why do they pounce upon the wing,
Save that they see and own their king ? "
 " Pshaw ! " said the farmer : " lump of pride !
They only follow to deride ;
Your scream affrights the evening hour,
When nightingales enchant the bower.
Why all on earth—man, beast, and fowl—
Know you for what you are—an owl.
You and your train ! 'midst Nature's rules,
Fools in derision follow fools ! "

FABLE XLII.

JUGGLER AND VICE.

A JUGGLER once had travelled thorough
Each city, market-town, and borough ;
You'd think, so far his art transcended,
Old Nick upon his fingers tended.
 Vice heard his name : she read his bill,
And sought his booth—defied his skill.
 The juggler, willing, laid a wager,
Not yet by losses rendered sager ;
He played his tricks of high emprize,—
Confounding touch, deluding eyes.

Then cards obeyed his will, and gold
From empty bags in torrents rolled!
He showed an ivory egg: and then
Hatched and brought forth the mother-hen!
   Vice then stepped forth, with look serene
Enough to stir a juggler's spleen:
She passed a magic looking-glass,
Which pleased alike dame, lad, and lass;
Whilst she, a senator addressing,
Said: "See this bank-note—lo! a blessing—
Breathe on it—Presto! hey! 'tis gone!"
And on his lips a padlock shone.
"Hey, presto!" and another puff,
It went, and he spoke well enough!
She placed twelve bottles on the board,
They were with some enchantment stored;
"Hey, presto!" and they disappear—
A pair of bloody swords were there.
She showed a purse unto a thief,
His fingers closed on it in brief;
"Hey, presto!" and—the treasure fled—
He grasped a halter, noosed, instead.
Ambition held a courtier's wand,
It turned a hatchet in his hand.
A box for charities, she drew;
"Blow here!" and a churchwarden blew—
"Hey, presto, open!" Opened, in her,
For gold was a parochial dinner!
Vice shook the dice, she smote the board,
And filled all pockets from her hoard.
A counter, in a miser's hand,
Grew twenty guineas at command;

She bade a rake to grasp them, fain—
They turned a counter back again.
The transmutations of a guinea
Made every one stare like a ninny ;
But fair was false, and false was fair,
By which Vice cheated eye and ear.
　　The juggler, though with grief at heart,
In recognition of her art,
Said : " Now and then I cheat the throng,
You every day—and all day long ! "

FABLE XLIII.

Council of Horses.

A STEED with mutiny inspired
The stud which grazed the mead, and fired
A colt, whose eyes then blazing fire,
Stood forth and thus expressed his ire :
　　" How abject is the equine race,
Condemned to slavery's disgrace !
Consider, friends, the deep reproach—
Harnessed to drag the gilded coach,
To drag the plough, to trot the road,
To groan beneath the pack-horse load !
Whom do we serve ?—a two-legged man,
Of feeble frame, of visage wan.
What ! must our noble jaws submit
To champ and foam their galling bit ?
He back and spur me ? Let him first
Control the lion—tiger's thirst :

I here avow that I disdain
His might, that I reject his reign.
He freedom claims, and why not we?
The nag that wills it, must be free!"

He paused: the intervening pause
Was followed by some horse-applause.

An ancient Nestor of the race
Advanced, with sober solemn pace;
With age and long experience wise,
He cast around his thoughtful eyes.
He said: "I was with strength endued,
And knew the tasks of servitude;
Now I am old—and now these plains
And grateful man, repay my pains.
I ofttimes marvelled to think, how
He knew the times to reap and plough;
And to his horses gave a share
Of the fair produce of the year.
He built the stable, stored the hay,
And winnowed oats from day to day.
Since every creature is decreed
To aid his brother in his need,
We served each other—horse and man—
And carried out the Eternal plan,
And each performed his part assigned:
Then calm your discontented mind."

The Nestor spoke—the colt submitted—
And, like his ancestry, was bitted.

FABLE XLIV.

HOUND AND HUNTSMAN.

SEEING yourselves are wise, ye smile
On fools and folly for a while;
But water wears the rocks, and sense
Is wearied by impertinence.
  The wind was southerly, the sky
Proclaimed that a good scent would lie—
Forth from the kennel burst the hounds,
As schoolboys sally out of bounds.
They hailed the huntsman; he by name
Greeted each dog, who thought it fame.
See them obey command: when bade,
They scattered thro' the copse and glade;
They snuffed the scent upon the gale,
And sought the remnant of a trail.
  Ringwood, a pup, on the alert,
Was very young and very pert;
He opened—from exuberant spirit—
But old dogs heard the puppy in it;
But when his note of " Full-cry " rose,
The huntsman to the puppy goes,—
Down falls the lash,—up rose the yelp,
And murmured thus the puppy whelp:
  " Why lash me? Are you malcontent
That I possess superior scent? "
  The huntsman answered: " Puppy slips
Must be restrained by lash of whips;
Puppies our scorn, not envy, raise —
For envy is akin to praise.

Had not that forward noisy tongue
The patience of your elders wrung,
You might have hunted with the pack ;
But now the whip assails your back :
You must be taught to know your ground,
And from a puppy grow a hound."

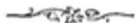

FABLE XLV.

ROSE AND POET.

I SCORN the man who builds his fame
On ruins of another's name :
As prudes, who prudishly declare
They by a sister scandaled are ;
As scribblers, covetous of praise,
By slandering, snatch themselves the bays ;
Beauties and bards, alike, are prone
To snatch at honours not their own.
As Lesbia listens, all the whister,
To hear some scandal of a sister.
How can soft souls, which sigh for sueings,
Rejoice at one another's ruins ?
  As, in the merry month of May,
A bard enjoyed the break of day,
And quaffed the fragrant scents ascending,
He plucked a blossomed rose, transcending
All blossoms else ; it moved his tongue
To rhapsodize, and thus he sung :

" Go, rose, and lie
On Chloë's bosom, and be there caressed ;
　　For there would I,
Like to a turtle-dove, aye flee to nest
　　From jealousy
And carking care, by which I. am opprest.
　　There lie—repose
Upon a bosom fragrant and as fair ;
　　Nor rival those
Beauties ethereal you discover there.
　　For wherefore, rose,
Should you, as I, be subject to despair?"

　"Spare your comparisons—oh! spare—
Of me and fragrancy and fair!"
A Maiden-blush, which heard him, said,
With face unwontedly flushed red.
" Tell me, for what committed wrong
Am I the metaphor of song?
I would you could write rhymes without me,
Nor in your ecstacies so flout me.
In every ditty must we bloom?
Can't you find elsewhere some perfume?
Oh! does it add to Chloë's sweetness
To visit and compare my meetness?
And, to enhance her face, must mine
Be made to wither, peak, and pine?"

F

FABLE XLVI.

CUR, HORSE, AND SHEPHERD'S DOG.

THE lad of mediocre spirit
Blurs not with modesty his merit.
On all exerting wit and tongue,
His rattling jokes, at random flung,
Bespatter widely friend and foe.
Too late the forward boy will know
That jokes are often paid in kind,
Or rankle longer in the mind.

   A village cur, with treble throat,
Thought he owned music's purest note,
And on the highway lay, to show it
Or to philosopher or poet.
Soon as a roadster's trot was heard,
He rose, with nose and ears upreared;
As he passed by assailed his heels,
Nor left him till they reached the fields.

   But, as it happened once, a pad,
Assailed by Master Snarl, like mad,
Flung out, and knocked him in the mire;
Nor did he stop to care, inquire,
If he had hurt him. On his way
Pad passed, and puppy bleeding lay.

   A shepherd's dog, who saw him bleed,
Who hated Snarl and all his breed,
Said, "This was brought about by prate,
Which horses—even horses—hate!"

FABLE XLVII.

THE COURT OF DEATH.

ONCE on a time, in solemn state,
Death, in his pomp of terror, sate.
Attendant on his gloomy reign,
Sadness and Madness, Woe and Pain,
His vassal train. With hollow tone
The tyrant muttered from his throne :
  "We choose a minister to-night ;
Let him who wills prefer his right,
And unto the most worthy hand
We will commit the ebon wand."
  Fever stood forth : "And I appeal
To weekly bills to show my zeal.
Repelled, repulsed, I persevere ;
Often quotidian through a year."
  Gout next appeared to urge his claim
For the racked joints of tortured frame :
He, too, besieged the man oppressed,
Nor would depart, although suppressed.
  Then Rheumatics stept forth, and said :
"I plague them as they lie in bed."
  Whilst Palsy said : "I make them stumble ;
When they get up, I make them tumble."
  Then quick Consumption, slow Decline,
Put in their claims, on counts malign ;
And Plague preferred his rapid power
To weed a nation in an hour.
  At the first pause, the monarch said :
" Merit of modesty was bred.

F 2

Does no physician strive with these?
Physicians are content with fees.
I say, give Drunkenness the wand;
There, give it to his drunken hand.
For wary men, as foes, detest
You, Rheumatics—who break their rest—
Fever, and Gout, who here contend;
But Drunkenness they think their friend,
Invite him to their feasts: he shares
Alike their merriments and cares.
He for another *magnum* calls
At weddings, births, and funerals."

FABLE XLVIII.

FLORIST AND PIG.

A FLORIST—wit had run a rig—
Had set his fancy on a pig;
Which followed master like a dog,
And petted was, although a hog.
　The master thus addressed the swine:
" My house and garden both be thine;
Feast on potatoes as you please,
And riot 'midst the beans and peas;
Turnips and carrots, pig, devour,
And broccoli and cauliflower;
But spare my tulips—my delight,
By which I fascinate my sight."
　But Master Pig, next morning, roamed
Where sweet wort in the coolers foamed.

He sucked his fill; then munched some grains,
And, whilst inebriated, gains
The garden for some cooling fruits,
And delved his snout for tulip-roots.
He did, I tell you, much disaster;
So thought, at any rate, his master:
" My sole, my only, charge forgot,
You drunken and ungrateful sot!"

  " Drunken, yourself!" said Piggy-wiggy;
" I ate the roots, not flowers, you priggy!"
  The florist hit the pig a peg,
And piggy turned and tore his leg.
  " Fool that I was," the florist said,
" To let that hog come near my bed!
Who cherishes a brutal mate,
Will mourn the folly, soon or late."

FABLE XLIX.

Man and Flea.

Nothing, methinks, is to be seen
On earth that does not overween.
Doth not the hawk, from high, survey
The fowls as destined for his prey?
And do not Cæsars, and such things.
Deem men were born to slave for kings?
The crab, amidst the golden sands
Of Tagus, or on pearl-strewn strands,
Or in the coral-grove marine,
Thinks hers each gem of ray serene.

The snail, 'midst bordering pinks and roses,
Where zephyrs fly and love reposes,
Where Laura's cheek vies with the peaches,
When Corydon one glance beseeches,—
The snail regards both fruit and flower,
And thanks God for the granted bower.
    And man, who, standing on some bluff,
Regards the world with soul as tough,—
The sun, the moon, the starry sphere,
The harvests of the circling year,
The mighty ocean, meadows trim,
And deems they all are made for him.
"How infinite," he says, "am I!
How wondrous in capacity!
Over creation to hold reign,
The lord of pleasure and of pain——"
    "Hold hard, my hearty!" said a flea,
Perched on his neck, beneath his lee.
"I do not brag that all creation
Is subject to the Flea-ite nation.
I know that parasitic races,
The Ticks and Lucies have their places;
But the imperial race of Flea
Is all surpassing—look at me.
My concentrated vigour, grant,
Then look at yon huge elephant;
Look at my leap, at my proboscis,
Then go and learn, ' UT TU TE NOSCIS,'
That man was made with skin to bleed,
That families of fleas may feed."

FABLE L.

HARE AND MANY FRIENDS.

FRIENDSHIP, as love, is but a name,
Save in a concentrated flame;
And thus, in friendships, who depend
On more than one, find not one friend.
   A hare who, in a civil way,
Was not dissimilar to GAY,
Was well known never to offend,
And every creature was her friend.
As was her wont, at early dawn,
She issued to the dewy lawn;
When, from the wood and empty lair,
The cry of hounds fell on her ear.
She started at the frightful sounds,
And doubled to mislead the hounds;
Till, fainting with her beating heart,
She saw the horse, who fed apart.
"My friend, the hounds are on my track;
Oh, let me refuge on your back!"
   The horse responded: "Honest Puss,
It grieves me much to see you thus.
Be comforted—relief is near;
Behold, the bull is in the rear."
   Then she implored the stately bull,
His answer we relate in full:
"Madam, each beast alive can tell
How very much I wish you well;
But business presses in a heap,
I an appointment have to keep;

And now a lady 's in the case,—
When other things, you know, give place.
Behold the goat is just behind ;
Trust, trust you'll not think me unkind."
  The goat declared his rocky lairs
Wholly unsuited were to hares.
"There is the sheep," he said, "with fleece.
Adapted, now, to your release."
  The sheep replied that she was sure
Her weight was too great to endure ;
"Besides," she said, "hounds worry sheep."
  Next was a calf, safe in a keep :
"Oh, help me, bull-calf—lend me aid!"
  "My youth and inexperience weighed,"
Replied the bull-calf, "though I rue it,
Make me incompetent to do it ;
My friends might take offence. My heart—
You know my heart, my friend—we part,
I do assure you——Hark! adieu!
The pack, in full cry, is in view."

FABLE LI.

Dog and Fox.

(To a Lawyer).

My friend, the sophisticated tongue
Of lawyers can turn right to wrong ;
And language, by your skill made pliant,
Can save an undeserving client.

Is it the fee directs the sense
To injure injured innocence?
Or can you, with a double face
Like Janus's, mistate a case?
Is scepticism your profession,
And justice absent from your session?
And is, e'en so, the bar supplied,
Where eloquence takes either side?

A man can well express his meaning,
Except in law deeds, where your gleaning
Must be first purchased—must be fee'd;
Engrossed, too, the too-prolix deed.
But do we shelter beneath law?
Ay, till your brother finds the flaw.
All wills pass muster, undisputed;
Dispute, and they are soon confuted:
And you, by instinct, flaws discover,
As dogs find coveys in the clover.

Sagacious Porta loved to trace
Likeness to brutes in lordly face—
To ape or owls his sketches liking,
Sent the laugh round—they were so striking.
So would I draw my satire true,
And fix it on myself or you.

But you dissent: you do not like
A portrait that shall rudely strike.
You write no libels on the state,
And party prejudice you hate;
But to assail a private name
You shrink, my friend, and deem it shame.
So be it: yet let me in fable
Knock a knave over, if I am able.

Shall not the decalogue be read,
Because the guilty sit in dread?
Brutes are my theme: am I to blame
If minds are brutish, men the same?
Whom the cap fits, e'en let him wear it—
And we are strong enough to bear it.

A shepherd's dog, unused to sporting,
Picked up acquaintance, all consorting.
Amongst the rest, a friendship grew
'Twixt him and Reynard, whom he knew.

Said Reynard: "'Tis a cruel case
That man will stigmatize my race:
Ah! there are rogues midst men and foxes—
You see that where the parish stocks is.
Still there are honest men and true—
So are there honest foxes too.
You see and know I've no disguise,
And that, like life, I honour prize."

The honest dog threw off distrust,
For talk like that seemed good and just.
On as they went one day with chatter
Of honour and such moral matter,
They heard a tramp. "Are hounds abroad?
I heard a clatter on the road."

"Nay," said the dog: "'tis market-day,
Dame Dobbin now is on her way.
That foot is Dun's, the pyebald mare:
They go to sell their poultry ware."

"Their poultry ware! Why poultry me?
Sir, your remark is very free.
Do I know your Dame Dobbin's farm?
Did I e'er do her hen-roost harm?"

" Why, my good friend, I never meant
To give your spirit discontent.
No lamb—for aught I ever knew—
Could be more innocent than you."

   " What do you mean by such a flam?
Why do you talk to me of lamb?
They lost three lambs : you say that I—
I robbed the fold ;--you dog, you lie !"

   " Knave," said the dog, " your conscience tweaks :
It is the guilty soul that speaks."
So saying, on the fox he flies,
The self-convicted felon dies.

———

FABLE LII.

VULTURE, SPARROW, AND BIRDS.

ERE I begin I must premise
Our ministers are good and wise :
Therefore if tongues malicious fly,
Or what care they, or what care I ?

   If I am free with courts, and skittish,
I ne'er presume to mean the British :
I meddle with no state affairs,
But spare my jest and save my ears ;
And our court schemes are too profound
For Machiavel himself to sound.
A captious fool may feel offended ;
They are by me uncomprehended.

   Your younger brother wants a place—
(That's many a younger brother's case).

You likewise tell me he intends
To try the court and beat up friends.
I trust he may a patriot find,
True to his king and to mankind,
And true to merit—to your brother's—
And then he need not teaze us others.
　　You praise his probity and wit:
No doubt; I doubt them not a whit.
Ah! may our patriot have them too;
And if both clash, why things may do.
For I have heard (oh, Heaven defend us!
For I'll not hold it might not mend us)
That ministers, high as yon steeple,
Have trodden low law, king, and people,
When virtue from preferment barred
Gets nothing save its own regard.
Courtiers—a set of knaves—attend them,
And arrogance well recommends them;
Who flatter them defame their foes
To lull the ministerial woes:
And if projectors fire a brain,
South Sea or silver mines in Spain,
The broker's ready in a trice
To satisfy e'en avarice.
A courtier's conscience must be pliant;
He must go on, nor be defiant,
Through thick and thin, o'er stock and stone,
Or else, bye, bye, the post is gone.
Since plagues like these as storms may lower,
And favourites fall as falls the flower,
Good principles should not be steady,—
That is, at court, but ever ready

To veer—as veers the vane—each hour
Around the ministry in power:
For they, you know, they must have tools;
And if they can't get knaves, get fools.
Ah! let me shun the public hate,
And flee the guilt of guilty state.
Give me, kind Heaven, a private station,
A mind serene for contemplation;
And if bright honour may be mine,
Profit and title I resign.
Now read my fable, and—in short,
Go, if you will, then—go to court.

   In days of yore (for cautious rhymes
Should aye eschew the present times)
A greedy vulture, skilled in preying,
Approached the throne, his wings displaying,
And at the royal eagle's ear
Burthens of state proposed to bear.
Behold him minister of state;
Behold his feathered throng await;
Behold them granting posts and places
Concordant with their worth and races.
The nightingales were all turned out,
And daws put in. " These birds, no doubt,
The vulture said, "are the most fit
Both for capacity and wit,
And very docile: they will do
My business, as I wish them to.
And hawk—the hawk is a good fellow—
And chanticleer, with cockscomb yellow;
But all the ravens—they must go—
Pry in futurities, you know.

That will not do; to baffle all
With truth, for the apocryphal.
No; jays and pies will do far better,—
They talk by rote, nor know a letter."

A sparrow, on the housetop, heard—
The sparrow is a knowing bird:
" If rogues unto preferments rise,
I ask nor place nor seignories.
To the thatched cottage, I, to find,
From courts afar, my peace of mind."

FABLE LIII.

APE AND POULTRY.

ESTEEM is frequently misplaced,
Where she may even stand disgraced;
We must allow to wealth and birth
Precedence, which is due on earth:
But our esteem is only due
Unto the worth of man and virtue.
Around an ancient pedigree
There is a halo fair to see,
With " unwrung withers " we afford
Our salutation to milord,
As due unto his ancient house,
Albeit his lordship be a chouse.
And riches dazzle us—we know
How much they might or should bestow;
But power is nothing, sans the will,
Often recalcitrant to ill:

And yet the mob will stand and gaze
On each, with similar amaze.
But worst of all the lot, we grant,
The parasite or sycophant:
Such as can vilely condescend
To dirty jobs; and bow and bend,
With meanest tropes of adulation,
To have and hold on to their station.
E'en such a ministry among
Are found amidst the waiting throng.
Where'er are misdeeds, there are bevies;
And wanting never at the levees,
Men who have trimmed the stocks, been rabbled,
In South Seas and in gold mines dabbled,
Where sycophants applauded schemes
Madder than the maddest madman's dreams.

When pagans sacrificed to Moloch,
They gave the first-born of their low stock;
But here, unless all history lies,
Nations are made the sacrifice.
For look through courts, and you will find
The principle that rules mankind,—
Worshipped beneath the sundry shapes
Of wolves, and lions, fox, and apes.

Where, then, can we esteem bestow,—
To-day in place, to-morrow low?
And the winged insects of his power
Gone—when they see the tempests lower:
Like to the bubble, full and fair,
With hues prismatic, puffed with air.
Another puff—and down it tends—
Earthward one dingy drop descends.

A maiden, much misused by Time—
All aspirations of her prime,
Like the soap bubble, puffed and burst,—
Monkeys, and dogs, and parrots nurst;
A whole menagerie employed
The passing hours which she enjoyed.
A monkey, big as a gorilla,
Who stalked beneath a big umbrella,
Was her prime minister : his finger
Was wont in each man's pie to linger.
She liked the monster, and assigned
The poultry-yard to him, to find
The daily rations of the corn.
Behold him now, with brow of scorn,
Amidst his vassals : come for picking—
Swans, turkeys, peacocks, ducks, and chicken.
The minister appeared, the crowd
Performed the reverence due ; and bowed
And spoke their compliments and duties,
Whilst he revolved in mind his new ties,
And thought " What is a place of trust?—
' And first unto thyself be just,
And then it follows that you can
Not be unjust to any man.'
That moral motto is most true ;
As Shakespeare teaches, will I do."
There was an applewoman's stall,
With plums and nuts, beneath a wall ;
With her he then proposed to trade,—
In corn, full payments to be made.
" Madam, in mind this dogma bear :
' Buy in the cheap ; sell in the dear ;'

And, since my barley costs me nothing,
My market is as cheap as stuffing."

    Away then went the stores of grain,—
The poultry died; and mistress, fain
To know the cause, named a commission—
Which ended in the Pug's dismission,
And left our hero in a hash,
With Newgate and refunded cash.

    A gander met him in disgrace,
Who knew him well when high in place.
"Two days ago," said Pug, "you bowed
The lowest of the cringing crowd."

    "I always bob my head before
I pass," said Goosey, "a barn-door.
I always cackle for my grain,
And so do all my gosling train:
But if I do not know a monkey,
Whene'er I see one,—I'm a donkey."

FABLE LIV.

ANT IN OFFICE.

You tell me that my verse is rough,
And to do mischief like enough;
Bid me eschew, in honest rhymes,
Follies of countries and crimes.
You ask me if I ever knew
Court chaplains thus lawn sleeves pursue?
I meddle not with gown or lawn;
I, therefore, have no need to fawn.

If they must soothe a patron's ear,
Not I—I was not born to bear;
All base conditions I refuse,
Nor will I so debase the muse.
　Though I ne'er flatter nor defame,
Yet would I fain bring guilt to shame;
And I corruption would expose,
Though all corrupted were my foes.
I no man's property invade,—
Corruption 's an unlawful trade;
So bribery also. Politicians
Should be tied down to such conditions;
If they were stinted of their tools,
Less were their train of knaves and fools.
　Were such the case, let us review
The dreadful mischiefs to ensue.
Some silver services 'twould stint,
But that would aggrandise the Mint;
Some ministers find less regard,
But bring their servants more reward;
Fewer informers, fewer spies,
But that would swell the year's supplies;
An annual job or two might drop,
We should not miss it 'midst the crop;
Some pensions, haply, be refused,
The Civil List be less abused;
It might the ministry confound,
And yet the State stand safe and sound.
Next, let it well be understood
I only mean my country's good—
I wish all courtiers did the same.
I wish to bar no honest claim;

I wish the nation out of debt;
No private man had cause to fret;
Yet law and public good to be
The pole-stars of the Ministry;
I wish corruption, bribery, pension,
Were things there were no need to mention:
I wish to strike a blow at vice,—
Fall where it may, I am not nice;
Although the Law—the devil take it!—
Can *scandalum magnatum* make it.
I vent no scandal, neither judge
Another's conscience; on I trudge,
And with my satire take no aim,
Nor knave nor steward name by name.
Yet still you think my fable bears
Allusion unto State affairs.

I grant it does so; but, what then?—
I strike at motives, not at men.
If hands corrupted harm the nation,
I bar no reader's application.

There was an Ant, of flippant tongue,
Who oft the ears of senates wrung;
Whether he knew the thing or no,
Assurance sat upon his brow;
Who gained the post whereto he strained—
The grain-controllership attained.
But then old laws were very strict,
And punished actions *derelict*.
Accounts were passed by year and year,
The auditors would then appear,
And his controllership of grain
Must his accounts and stock explain.

G 2

He put a balance-sheet in—*cooked*,
An honest emmet o'er it looked,
And said, "The hoard of grain is low;
But the accounts themselves don't show
By any vouchers what the stocks are.
Really, such documents but mocks are."
   "Sir," the controller said, "would you
Have us pass everything to view?
Divulge all matters to all eyes,
Proclaim to winds state mysteries?
'Twould lay us open to our foes;
You see all that we dare disclose;
And, on my honour, the expense
Is lavished on the swarm's defence."
   They passed the balance-sheet—again
Next year's shewed "deficit of grain;"
And thus again controller pleaded:
"Much secret service has been needed,
For famines threaten; turkey broods
Have been most clamorous for foods.
Turkey invasions have cost dear,
And geese were numerous last year.
Really, these secrets told are ruin,
And tend much to the realm's undoing."
   Again, without examination,
They thanked his good administration.
A third and fourth time this recurred,
An auditor would then be heard:
"Are we but tools," he said, "of rogues?
Through us corruption disembogues
Her mighty flood; for every grain
We touch we vouch at least for twain.

Where have they vanished? nay, in bribes.
They have depoverished our tribes."
  Then followed an investigation,
And a report unto the nation.
The Ant was punished, and his hoard—
All that remained of it—restored.

FABLE LV.

THE BEAR IN A BOAT.

(To a Coxcomb).

AH! my dear fellow, write the motto
NOSCE TEIPSUM o'er your grotto;
For he must daily wiser grow,
Determined his own scope to know.
He never launches from the shore
Without the compass, sail, and oar.
He, ere he builds, computes the costs;
And, ere he fights, reviews the hosts.
He safely walks within the fence,
And reason takes from common sense:
Pride and presumption standing checked
Before some palpable defect.
  To aid the search for pride's eviction,
A coxcomb claims a high distinction.
Not to one age or sex confined
Are coxcombs, but of rank and kind;

Pervading all ranks, great and small,
Who take and never give the wall.
By ignorance is pride increased ;
They who assume most, know the least.
Yet coxcombs do not, all alike,
Our ridicule and laughter strike.
For some are lovers, some are bores,
Some rummage in the useless stores
Of folios ranged upon the shelf,
Another only loves himself.
Such coxcombs are of private station :
Ambition soars to rule the nation.
They flattery swallow ; do not fear,—
No nonsense will offend their ear :
Though you be sycophant professed,
You will not put his soul to test.
If policy should be his care,
Drum MACHIAVELLI in his ear ;
If commerce or the naval service,
Potter of Mazarin and Jervis.
Always, with due comparison,
By him let all that's done be done :
Troops, levies, and ambassadors,
Treaties and taxes, wars and stores ;
No blunders or crude schemes are tost,
Each enterprise repays its cost.
He is the pilot at the helm
To succour and to save the realm.
Spare not your Turkey-poult to cram,
He never will suspect you *flam*.
    There was a bear of manners rough,
Who could take bee-hives well enough :

He lived by plundered honey-comb,
And raided the industrial home.
Success had puffed him with conceit;
He boasted daily of some feat.
In arrogance right uncontrolled
He grew pragmatic, busy, bold;
And beasts, with reverential stare,
Thought him a most prodigious bear.

   He grew dictator in his mood,
And seized on every spoil was good;
From chickens, rising by degrees,
Until he took the butcher's fees:
Then, in his overweening pride,
Over the hounds he would preside;
And, lastly, visiting the rocks,
He took his province from the fox.
And so it happened on a day
A yawl equipped at anchor lay.
He stopped, and thus expressed his mind:
" What blundering puppies are mankind!
What stupid pedantry in schools,
Their compasses and nautic tools!
I will assume the helm, and show
Vain man a dodge he ought to know."

   He gained the vessel, took his stand.
The beasts, astonished, lined the strand;
He weighed the anchor, slacked the sail,
Put her about before the gale,
But shipped no rudder: ill then met her;
He ran ashore, and there upset her.

   The roach and gudgeon, native there,
Gathered to quiz the floundering bear.

Not so the watermen: the crew
Gathered around to thrash him too;
And merriment ran on the strand
As Bruin, chained, was dragged to land.

FABLE LVI.

Squire and Cur.

(To a Country Gentleman).

Man, with integrity of heart,
Disdains to play a double part:
He bears a moral coat of mail,
When envy snarls and slanders rail.
From virtue's shield the shafts resound,
And his light shines in freedom round.
  If in his country's cause he rise,
Unbribed, unawed, he will advise;
Will fear no ministerial frown,
Neither will clamour put him down.
But if you play the politician
With soul averse to the position,
Your lips and teeth must be controlled.
  What minister his place could hold
Were falsehood banished from the court,
Or truth to princes gain resort?
The minister would lose his place,
If he could not his foes disgrace.
  For none is born a politician
Who cannot lie by intuition:

By which the safety of the throne
Is kept—subservient to his own.
For monarchs must be kept deluded
By falsehood from the lips exuded,
And, ministerial schemes pursuing,
Care nothing for the public ruin.

    Antiochus, lost in a chase,
Traversed the wood with mended pace,
And reached a cottage, sore distressed.
A Parthian fed the regal guest,
But knew not whom: the countryman,
Warmed by unwonted wine, began
To talk of courts and talk of kings:

    " We country folk, we see such things.
They say the king is good and wise:
Ah! we could open both his eyes.
They say, God bless him! he means good.
Ah! we could open them—we could ;—
And show him how his courtiers ride us:
They rob us, and they then deride us.
If King Antiochus could see,
Or if he knew as much as we,
How servants wound a master's name,—
From kings to cobblers 'tis the same,—
If King Antiochus, I say,
Could see, he'd kick those scamps away."

    Both in good time their couches sought ;
The peasant slept, the monarch thought.
At earliest dawn the courtiers found
And owned the king by trumpet sound.
Unto his rustic host the guest,
With due reward, his thanks expressed ;

And turning to his courtier train:
" Since you are bent on private gain,
You may your private gain pursue;
Henceforth I will be quit of you."

A country squire, by whim directed,
The nobler stocks canine neglected;
Nor hound nor pointer by him bred.
Yap was his cur, and Yap was fed;
And Yap brought all his blood relations
To fill the posts and eat the rations;
And to that end it came about
That all the others were turned out.
Now Yap, as curs are wont to do—
If great men's curs—on tradesmen flew,
Unless they bribed him: with a bound
He worried all the tenants round.
For why? he lived in constant fear
Lest they, in hate, should interfere.
So Master Yap would snarl and bite,
Then clap his tail, and fly with fright;
As he, with bay and bristling hair,
Assailed each tradesman who came there.
He deemed, if truth should get admittance,
'Twould followed be by his demittance.

It chanced that Yap, upon a day,
Was by a kins-cur lured to play;
And, as Miss Yaps there were, they thought
Unto Miss Yaps to pay their court,
And had a little hunting bouting,
Like Antony, who so went outing
With Cleopatra.—So pursuing,
Yap and Mark Antony found ruin.

A neighbour passing by, then ventured—
And, seeing the coast clear, he entered.
The squire enjoyed a quiet chat,
And said: "Now tell me, neighbour Mat,
Why do men shun my hall? Of late,
No neighbour enters in my gate;
I do not choose thence to infer ——"

  "Squire, 'tis nothing but the cur,"
Mat answered him; "with cursed spite,
The brute does nought but bark and bite.
There is some cause, we all agree:
He swears 'tis us—we say 'tis he.
Get rid of him, the snarling brute,
And these old halls shall not be mute;
There nothing is we more desire,
Than lose the cur and win the squire."

  The truth prevailed, and with disgrace
The cur was cudgelled out of place.

FABLE LVII.

The Countryman and Jupiter.

(To myself).

Nosce teipsum: look and spy,
Have you a friend so fond as I?
Have you a fault, to mankind known,
Not hidden unto eyes your own?

When airy castles you importune,
Down falling, by the breath of Fortune,
Did I e'er doubt you should inherit,
If Fortune's wheel devolved on merit?
It was not so; for Fortune's frown
Still perseveres to hold you down.
Then let us seek the cause, and view
What others say and others do.
Have we, like those in place, resigned
Our independency of mind?
Have we had scruples—and therefore
Practising morals, are we poor?
If such be our forlorn position,
Would Fortune mend the lorn condition?
On wealth if happiness were built,
Villains would compass it by guilt.
No: CRESCIT AMOR NUMMI—misers
Are not so heartwhole as are sizars.
Think, O John Gay!—and that 's myself—
Should Fortune make you her own elf,
Would that augment your happiness?
Or haply might she make it less?

   Suppose yourself a wealthy heir
Of houses, lands, and income clear:
Your luxury might break all bounds
Of plate and table, steeds, and hounds.
Debts—debts of honour—lust of play—
Will waste a county's wealth away;
And so your income clear may fail,
And end in exile or in jail.

   Or were you raised to height of power,
Would that ameliorate an hour?

Would avarice and false applause
Weigh in the balance as two straws?
Defrauded nations, blinded kings,
Would they not, think you, leave their stings?
If happiness, then, be your aim
(I mean the true, not false of fame),
She nor in courts nor camps resides,
Nor in the lowly cottage bides;
Nor on the soil, nor on the wind;
She tenants only in the mind.

   Wearied by toil, beneath the shade,
A rustic rested on his spade.
" This load of life, from year to year,"
He said, " is very hard to bear.
The dawning morning bids me up
To toil and labour till I sup ! "

   Jove heard, and answered him : " My friend,
Complaints that are unjust offend :
Speak out your griefs, if you repine
At any act or deed of mine.
If you can mend your state, instruct me ;
I wish but knowledge to conduct me."

   So saying, from the mundane crowds
He raised the rustic to the clouds.

   He showed a miser—said : " Behold
His bulky bags that burst with gold !
He counts it over, and the store
Is every day increased by more."

   " O happiness ! " the rustic cried :
" What can a fellow wish beside ? "

   " Ah, wait ! until I charm your eyes,"
Said Jupiter, " from fallacies."

He looked again, and saw the breast
Like a rough ocean—ne'er at rest:
Fear, guilt, and conscience gnawed the heart;
Extortion ever made it smart—
It seemed as if no sunlit gleam
Could brighten it in thought or dream.

   " Ah! may the gods," he cried, " reject
My prayer for gold, and comfort wreckt:
But see yon minister of state,
And the gay crowd who proudly wait!"

   " A second time I charm your eyes,"
Said Jove, " from mortal fallacies."

   He looked again, and saw a breast
Gnawed by corruption, wanting rest:
He saw him one time drunk with power,
Tottering upon Ambition's tower;
Then, seized with giddiness and fear,
Seeing his downfall in his rear,
" O Jupiter!" the rustic said,
" Give me again my plough and spade."

   But Jupiter was not contented;
The rustic's griefs he still resented.
So he deployed before his sight
The lawyer's and the soldier's plight;
The miseries of war and law,
The battle-field and legal flaw.

   " O Jupiter!" the rustic said,
Restore me to the plough and spade."

   Then Jupiter: " You mortals blunder:
There is no happiness in thunder;
For happiness, to nought confined,
Is found in the contented mind:

Go home again, and be contented,
Nor grumble more like one demented."
  Then Jupiter, to aid the clown,
Where he had found him put him down.

FABLE LVIII.

MAN, CAT, DOG, AND FLY.

(To my Native Land.)

MY native land, whose fertile ground
Neptune and Amphitritè bound,—
Britain, of trade the chosen mart,
The seat of industry and art,—
May never luxury or minister
Cast over thee a mantle sinister!
Still let thy fleet and cannon's roar
Affright thy foes and guard thy shore.
When Continental States contend,
Be thou to them a common friend.
Imperial rule may sway their land;
Here Commerce only takes her stand,
Diffusing good o'er all the world.
The flag of Commerce, where unfurled,
Stands with fair plenty in her train,
And wealth, to bless her bright domain.
For where the merchant sails to trade
Fair is the face of Nature made.
Glad is the king, in regal dome;
Glad is the rustic, in his home;

The flocks and culture glad the fields,
And Peace her boon of plenty yields.
For Nature meant that man should share
The goods abounding everywhere,
And barter corn, and oil, and wine;
The iron ore and twisted twine,
Cotton and silk, deep-bedded coal,
Be interchanged from pole to pole.
So each land's superfluities
Should bind lands by commercial ties;
And carry, from abounding stores,
The luxuries of distant shores.
The monarch and the rustic eat
Of the same harvest, the same wheat;
The artizan supplies the vest,
The mason builds the roof of rest;
The self-same iron-ores afford
The coulter of the plough and sword;
And all, from cottage to the throne,
Their common obligation own
For private and for public cause,
Protecting property and laws.
  The animals were once distressed
By bitter famine, and addressed
Themselves to man to find them food,
And bound themselves in servitude;
For, whilst they starved, or whilst they fed,
Man had his lasting hoards of bread.
  The cat demanded leave to sue.
" Well, Puss," says Man, "and what can you do?"
" Scatter the rats and mice," said Tib;
" And guard your grain in sack or crib.

Foe am I of the *genus Mus*,
Absurdly called '*ridiculus*;'
Dan Æsop called him so, not I;
Feed me, and every mouse shall die."
  Then to the starving hound, Man said:
" Well, sir, and how can you earn bread?"
  "My name is Trusty," said the hound;
And ne'er was I untrusty found.
I am not used, by self-applause,
To pander to my famished jaws;
But I am well known; if you please
To ask my character of these.
My province is to watch, and keep
The house and fold the whilst you sleep;
And thief and wolf alike shall know
I am your friend, and am their foe."
  " Ah!" said the Man, "we rarely find
Trust uncorrupted with mankind.
Such services, indeed, transcend;
Pray, be my comrade and my friend."
  Then to the drone he turned, and said:
" Well, sir; can you, sir, earn your bread?"
  " I will explain, sir, if I can;
I am," said drone, " a gentleman.
Mechanics earn their bread—not I:
Where'er there honey is, I fly;
But, truly, it would not be fit
I should submit to toil for it:
I visit peaches, plums, and roses,
Where Beauty on a couch reposes;
I seldom fail the placid hour,
When she takes bohea in the bower;

H

Nor do I gather stores of pelf—,
My object is to please myself;
And if I lay to aught pretence,
It is to ease and elegance."
　"So, Mr. Drone; and have you done?
Then, from that peach, I pray, begone;
If you won't work, you shall not eat,—
That is, with me; so quit that seat.
If all the world were such as you,
We all should starve when north winds blew.
But he who, with industrious zeal,
Contributes to the common weal,
Has the true secret understood
Of private and of public good.
Be off with you!"　He raised his hand,
Which the vain insect dared withstand;
It smote the parasite of pride
And there the idler fell, and died.

FABLE LIX.

THE JACKALL, LEOPARD, AND BEASTS.

(To a Modern Politician.)

I GRANT these facts: corruption sways,
Self-interest does pervert man's ways;
That bribes do blind; that present crimes
Do equal those of former times:
Can I against plain facts engage
To vindicate the present age?

I know that bribes in modern palm
Can nobler energies encalm;
That where such argument exists
There itching is in modern fists.
And hence you hold that politicians
Should drive their nails on such conditions,
So they might penetrate *sans* bending,
And win your way past comprehending.

   Premising no reflection 's meant,
Unto such doctrine I dissent.
The barrister is bound to plead
Upon the side on which he 's fee'd;
And so in every other trade
Is duty, by the guinea, paid.
Man, we are taught, is prone to evil—
That does not vindicate the devil:
Besides, man, in his own behoof,
Contrives to hide the cloven hoof.
Nor is corruption of late date,—
'Twas known in every age and state;
And where corruption was employed
The public welfare was destroyed.

   Next see court minions in disgrace,
Stripped of their treasure, stripped of place;
What now is all their pride and boast,—
The servile slave, the flattering host,
The tongues that fed him with applause,
The noisy champions of their cause?
They press the foremost to accuse
His selfish jobs and paltry views.
Ah, me! short-sighted were the fools,
And false, aye false, the hireling tools.

Was it such sycophants to get
Corruption swelled the public debt?
This motto would not shine amiss—
Write, " Point d'argent et point de Suisse."
   The lion is the noblest brute,
With parts and valour past dispute,
And yet it is by all averred
His rule to jackalls is transferred.
   A rascal jackall once on law
And property put down his paw.
The forest groaned brute-discontent,
And swore its injuries to resent:
The jackall heard it, and with fear
He saw disgrace approaching near.
   He said and thought: " I must defeat
Malicious tongues, and guard my seat;
Strengthen myself with new allies,
And then this clamour may despise."
Unto the generous brutes he fawned;
The generous brutes the jackall scorned.
What must he do? Friends must be made,
And proselytes by bribes be paid;
For think not a brute's paw withstands
The bribe which dirties human hands.
   A hog o'er cabbage said his benison;
The wolf was won by haunch of venison;
A pullet won the fox; a thistle
Tickled the donkey's tongue of gristle.
   But now the royal leopard rose
The tricksy jackall to oppose:
And as the rats will leave in lurch
The falling walls of house or church,

So did each briber cut and run
To worship at the rising sun.
The hog with warmth expressed his zeal,
So did the wolf for public weal,—
But claimed their venison and cabbage.
The fox the like—without disparage
Unto his perquisites of geese.
The donkey asked a common's lease.
  " Away," the leopard said, " ye crew,
Whose conscience honesty ne'er knew !
Away, I say, with all the tribe
Who dare to ask or take a bribe:
Cudgels, and not rewards, are due
To such time-serving tools as you !"

FABLE LX.

The Degenerate Bees.

(To Dean Swift.)

Though courts the practice disallow,
I ne'er a friend will disavow:
It may be very wrong to know him,
And very prudent to forego him;
'Tis said that prudence changes friends
Oft as it suits one's private ends.
Ah, Dean ! and you have many foes,
Behind, before, beneath your nose,—

And fellows very high in station,
Of high and low denomination,
Who dread you with a deadly spite
For what you speak and what you write,—
Where, between satire and your wit,
They feel themselves most sorely bit.
Ah! can a dunce in church or state
So overflow with froth and hate?
And can a scribbling crew so spurt
On Pope and Swift, who stand unhurt?

   Ah! can it be, a mighty race
(For giants may hold power and place)
Can scandals raise and libels pen
To prove that they are worthy men?
They suffered from your pen, 'tis true,
Therefore you have from them your due.
You have no friends—be it understood
Except myself—and wise and good.
To lay the matter on the table,
And give it point, I'll tell a fable.

   A bee, who greedy was of gain,
But wanted parts him to maintain,
Seeing small rogues by great ones thrive,
Corruption sowed throughout the hive.
And as he rose in power and place
Importance settled on his face;
All conscience found with him discredit,
But impudence the loudest—merit:
Wealth claimed distinction and found grace,
But poverty was ever base.
Right, law, and industry gave way
Where'er his selfish rule had sway;

And so corruption seized the swarm,
Who plundered underneath his arm.
Thus he harangued : " Whilst vulgar souls
Waste life in low mechanic holes,
Let us scorn drudgery : the drone
And wasp, whose elegance we own,
Like gentlemen sport in the rays
Of sunbeams on all summer days ;
It were not fitting they should moil,—
They live upon their neighbour's toil."

A bee, with indignation warm,
Stepped forth from the applauding swarm :
" The laws our native hives protect,
And for the laws bees hold respect.
I do not mind your frown ; I cry—
Bees live by honest industry.
'Twas toil and honest gain to thrive,
Which gave us an ancestral hive,
Which gave us our time-honoured dome,
Bequeathed with store of honeycomb.
Pursue the self-same road to fame
By which your fathers won their name :
But know the road you are pursuing
Will lead you to the brink of ruin."

He spoke ; but he was only hissed,
And from his cell forthwith dismissed.
With him* two other friends resigned,
Indignant at the Apian mind.
" These drones, who now oppress the State,
Proclaim our virtue by their hate,"

---

* Lords Oxford and Bolingbroke, in 1714, are intended.

The exile said; " our honest zeal
Will serve again the common weal;
And we, be sure, shall be replaced,
When they shall from this hive be chased."

FABLE LXI.

THE PACK-HORSE AND THE CARRIER.

(To a Young Nobleman.)

BEGIN, my lord, in early youth,
To bear with, nay encourage, truth.
And blame me not, for disrespect,
That I the flatterer's style reject.

 Let Virtue be your first pursuit;
Is not the tree known by its fruit?
Set your great ancestry in view;
Honour the title from them due.
Assert that you are nobly born,
Viewing ignoble things with scorn.

 My lord, your ancestry had not
The wealth and heirlooms you have got;
Yet was their conscience aye their own,
Nor ever pandered to the throne.
With hands by no corruption stained
They ministerial bribes disdained;
They served the Crown, upheld the laws,
And bore at heart their country's cause:
So did your sires adorn their name,
And raised the title unto fame.

My lord, 'tis not permitted you
To do what humbler men may do.
You may not be a dunce : your post
Is foremost, and before the host.
You may not serve a private end ;
To jobs you may not condescend ;
As from obscurity exempt,
So are you open to contempt.
Your name alone descends by birth,
Your fame is consequent on worth ;
Nor deem a coronet can hide
Folly or overweening pride :
Learning, by toil and study won,
Was ne'er entailed from sire to son.
If you degenerate from your race,
Its merit heightens your disgrace.

   A carrier, at night and morn,
Watched while his horses ate their corn :
It sunk the ostler's vales, 'tis true ;
But then his horses got their due.
It were as well, in some like cases,
If Ministers watched over places.

   And as he stood, the manger minding,
And heard the teeth continue grinding,
There was a racket ; for a pack-horse
Foamed at the mouth, and was in rack hoarse.

   "Why, zounds !" he cried ; "where have I got?
Is, then, my high descent forgot?
Must I endure the vile attacks
Of carriers' drudges—common hacks ?
May Roan and Dobbin poke their noses
In cribs where my great nose reposes?

Good gracious me! why, here's old Ball!—
No longer sacred is the stall.
I see Democracy and Devil
Will soon put all upon one level.
We have not been of race of Could-would,
At Epsom, Newmarket, and Goodwood;
Nor, by Dame Truth! I vow and pledge her,
Are we unknown at the St. Leger.
Unnumbered are our triumphs, told;
Unnumbered are the cups we hold;
Unnumbered are our laurels won;
And am I to be put upon
By carrier-nags of low degree?
O Fortune, do not let it be!"
  "You stupid blockhead!" said the carrier;
" 'Twixt you and us there is no barrier.
Your headstrong youth and wilful heart
Reduced you to a servile part;
And every carrier on the road
Avers your oats are ill-bestowed.
But, know that you do not inherit
From dam or sire any merit.
We give your ancestors their due,
But any ass is good as you.
As you are asinine and crass,
So do we treat you—as an ass."

FABLE LXII.

PAN AND FORTUNE.

(*To a Young Heir.*)

No sooner was thy father's death
Proclaimed to some, with bated breath,
Than every gambler was agog
To win your rents and gorge your prog.
  One counted how much income clear
You had in " ready "—by the year.
  Another cast his eyelid dark
Over the mansion and the park.
Some weighed the jewels and the plate,
And all the unentailed estate :
So much in land from mortgage free,
So much in personality.
  Would you to highwaymen abroad
Display your treasures on the road ?
Would you abet their raid of stealth
By the display of hoarded wealth ?
And are you yet with blacklegs fain
With loaded dice to throw a main ?
It is not charity—for shame !
The rascals look on you as game.
And you—you feed the rogues with bread—
By you rascality is fed.
Nay, more, you of the gallows cheat
The scoundrels who would be its meat.
The risks of the highway they shun,
Having your rents to prey upon.

Consider, ere you lose the bet,
That you might pay your duns and debt.
Consider, as the dice-box rattles,
Your honour and unpaid for chattels.
Think of to-morrow and its duns;
Usurious interest, how it runs;
And scoundrel sharpers, how they cheat you.
Think of your honour, I entreat you.

Look round, and see the wreck of play,—
Estate and honour thrown away:
Their one time owner, unconfined,
Wanders in equal wreck of mind,
Or tries to learn the trade by which
He ruined fell, and so grow rich:
But failing there, for want of cunning,
Subsists on charity by dunning.
Ah! you will find this maxim true:—
" Fools are the game which knaves pursue."

And now the sylvans groan: the wood
Must make the gamester's losses good.
The antique oaks, the stately elms,
One common ruin overwhelms.
The brawny arms of boor and clown
Cast with the axe their honours down,
With Echo's repetitive sounds
Complaining of the raided bounds.

Pan dropt a tear, he hung his head,
To see such desolation spread.
He said: " To slugs I hatred bear,
To locusts that devour the ear,
To caterpillars, fly, and lice;
But what are they to cursed dice?

Or what to cards? A bet is made,
Which ruin is to mount or glade;
My glory and my realm defaced,
And my best regions run to waste.
It is that hag's—that Fortune's—doing:
She ever meditates my ruin.
False, fickle jade! who more devours
Than frost, in merry May, eats flowers."
　　But Fortune heard Pan railing thus.
" Old Pan," said Fortune, " what 's this fuss?
Am I the patroness of dice?
Is not she our fair cousin, Vice?
Do I cog dice or mark the cards?
Do gamesters offer me regards?
They trust to their own fingers' ends:
On Vice, not me, the game depends.
So would I save the fools, if they
Would not defy my rule by play.
They worship Folly,—and the knaves
Own all her votaries for slaves.
They cast their elm and oak trees low:
'Tis Folly,—Folly is thy foe.
Dear Pan, then do not rail on me:
I would have saved him every tree."

FABLE LXIII.

Plutus, Cupid, and Time.

Of all the burthens mortals bear
Time is most galling and severe;

Beneath his grievous load oppressed
We daily meet a man distressed:
" I've breakfasted, and what to do
I do not know; we dine at two."
He takes a pamphlet or the papers,
But neither can dispel his vapours;
He raps his snuff-box, hums an air,
He lolls, or changes now his chair,
He sips his tea, or bites his nails,
Then finds a chum, and then bewails
Unto his sympathising ear
The burthen they have both to bear.
  " I wish all hours were *post meridiem*,"
Said Tom; " so that I were well rid of 'm.
Why won't men play piquet and ombre
Before the evening hour grows sombre?
The women do it,—play quadrille
Morning and evening when they will.
They cast away the spleen and vapours
By daylight as by midnight tapers."
  " My case is different," said Will;
" I have the means, but lack the skill:
I am a courtier, in attendance,
And sleep the time out in dependence.
I should have been until the dark,
But for this rain now, in the park,
And then at court, till coming night
Puts court and all my cares to flight.
Then comes my dinner: then away
From wine unto the stupid play
Till ten o'clock; and then assemblies.
And so my time, which you contemn, flies.

I like to ramble midst the fair,
And nothing I find vexes there,—
Save that time flies: and then the club
Gives men their supper and their rub.
And there we all enjoy ourselves,
Till slumber lays us on her shelves."

My worthy friends, Time which devours,
Eats up the demons—passing hours:
Were you to books or business bred,
Too fleetly, then, would they be sped;
For time is fugitive as air.
Now lay aside your spleen or care,
And listen unto me and fable—
That is to say, if you are able.

Plutus, one morn, met Master Cupid;
They stood a moment, as though stupid,
Until they recognised each other.
They complimented with some pother,
When Time overtook them in his walk,
And then all three fell into talk
Of what each one had done for man.
And Plutus, purse-proud, he began :.

" Let kings or cobblers, for that matter,
Tell of the gifts which we bespatter;
Deem ye, that loyalty encumbers
The congregated courtly numbers?
Be undeceived : the strongest hold
Man has on fellow-man is gold !
Knaves have led senates, swayed debates,
Enriched themselves, and beggared states.
Flatter yourselves no more : 'tis riches—
The depth of pocket of the breeches—

That rules the roast. Unhappy wight
Is the poor soul with pocket light;
His solitary day descends,
Quite unencumbered by his friends."
  "Of human hearts, and of their yearnings,"
Said Cupid, " I have some discernings;
And own the power of gold. Its power,
Added to beauty as its dower,
Has oftentimes—there's no disputing—
Added a charm, was passed confuting.
Ay—marriage, as has been professed,
Is but a money-job at best;
But not so hearts, and not so love,—
They are the power of gold above.
Those who have true love known and tried,
Have every pettier want defied;
They nestle, and, beneath the storm,
In their own love lie snug and warm.
They every selfish feeling smother,
And one lives only for the other."
  Then Time, who pulled his forelock, said:
" To love and money man is wed,
And very apt are both to flout me;
And, if they could, would do without me.
Fools! I supply the vital space
In which they move, and run their race;
Without me they would be a dream.
Behold the miser! does he deem
Those hoards are his? So long—no more—
Than I am with him, is the store.
Soon from him as I pass away,
His heir will lavish them with play.

To arts and learning, matins' chime,
Vespers and midnight, seizing time,
I never know an idle hour—
Love not more fugitive in bower.
But I have heard coquettes complain
That they have let the seasons wane,
Nor caught me in my flight; and sorrowed
To see the springtide was but borrowed—
Not permanent—and so had wasted
The tide of joy they never tasted.
But myriads have their time employed,
And myriads have their time enjoyed.
Why then are mortals heedless grown,
Nor care to make each hour their own?
They should beware how we may sever,
At unawares, once and for ever!"
   Cupid and Plutus understood
Old Time was man's supremest good:
To him they yielded, and confessed
Time is of godlike blessings—best.

FABLE LXIV.

Owl, Swan, Cock, Spider, Ass, and Farmer.

(To a Mother.)

Yes, I have seen your eyes maternal
Beam, as beam forth the stars eternal,
Intercommuning of your joys—
Sayings and doings of your boys.

Nature, in body and in mind,
Has been to them profusely kind;
It now remains to do your part,
To sow good morals in the heart.
None other, as a mother can,
Can form and educate the man.
Perhaps now you anticipate
In youth unknown each future state.
The Church, the Navy, and the Bar,
I censure not: such choices are
Precarious truly in the event;
Yet ere we give a last assent,
We should remember nor destroy
The latent genius in the boy.
　　Martial relates—a father once
Wrote thus about his boy, a dunce:
" You know I've stuck at no expense
To train the lad, and rouse his sense;
To me it seems he backward goes
Like to a crab—for aught he knows.
My friend, advise me what to do."
And Martial thus replied in few:
" Make him a grazier or a drover,
And let him dwell in rural clover."
'Tis doubtful if the father heard
This answer—he returned no word.
　　The urchin, wanting wit, is sent
To school to grow impertinent;
To college next; which left, he blunders
In law, or military thunders;
Or, if by medical degree,
The sexton shares the doctor's fee,

Or, if for orders passed, as full fit,
He only potters from the pulpit,
We see that Nature has been foiled
Of her intent—a tradesman spoiled.
And even so do Ministers
Reward with places human burrs;
For it is very meet and fit
They should reward their kinsman's wit.
Are such times past?   Does merit now
In a due course and channel flow?
Distinguished in their posts, do we
Worth and desert rewarded see?
Survey the reverend bench, and spy
If patrons choose by piety?
Is honesty, disgraced and poor,
Distinct from what it was of yore?
And are all offices no longer
Granted unto the rich and stronger?
And are they never held by sparks,
With all the business done by clerks?
Do we, now, never contemplate
Appointments such, in Church and State?
And is there in no post a hobbler,
Who should have been, by right, a cobbler?
Patrons, consider such creations
Expose yourselves and your relations;
You should, as parents to the nation,
Ponder upon such nomination—
And know, whene'er you wield a trust,
Your judgment ever should be just.
   An owl of magisterial air,
Of solemn aspect, filled the chair;

And, with the port of human race,
Wore wisdom written on his face.
He from the flippant world retired,
And in a barn himself admired;
And, like an ancient sage, concealed
The follies foppish life revealed.
He pondered o'er black-lettered pages
Of old philosophers and sages—
Of Xenophon, and of the feat
Of the ten thousand in retreat;
Pondered o'er Plutarch and o'er Plato,
On Scipio, Socrates, and Cato.
But what most roused the bird's conceit,
Was Athens—academic seat—
From which he thought himself descended.
He an academy attended,
And learnt by rote dogmatic rules;
And, with trite sentences for tools,
He opened an academy—
Himself the *Magister* to be:
And it won fame. The stately swan
There sent her son and heir; her son
Dame Partlet sent; and Mister Spider,
Who in mechanics levelled wider;
And Sir John Asinus, with hopes
On music, metaphors, and tropes.
With years, their education done
And life before them to be run,
The mothers Dr. Owl consulted
On their career—and this resulted:
The swan was to the army sent;
The cock unto the navy went;

The spider went to Court; and Neddy
For Handel's music was made ready.
They played their parts, the public railed:
They, spite of education, failed.
  " You blockhead ! " said an honest farmer,
Who grew with indignation warmer,
" You are an owl : and are as blind,
As parents, to the youthful mind.
Had you with judgment judged, the swan
Had his career in nautics ran ;
The cock had played the soldier's part.
The spider plied the weaver's art ;
And for the donkey, dull and crass,
You should have let him be an ass.

FABLE LXV.

COOKMAID, TURNSPIT, AND OX.

(*To a Poor Man.*)

CONSIDER man in every sphere,
Then answer,—Is your lot severe?
Is God unjust? You would be fed :
I grant you have to toil for bread.
Your wants are plainly to you known,
So every mortal feels his own ;
Nor would I dare to say I knew,
'Midst men, one happier man than you,
  Adam in Paradise was lone ;
With Eve was first transgression known ;

And thus they fell, and thus disgrace
Entailed the curse on human race.
  When Philip's son, by glory fired,
The empire of the world desired,
He wept to find the course he ran—
Despite of altars—was of man.
So avaricious hopes are checked,
And so proud man may lack respect;
And so ambition may be foiled
Of the reward for which it moiled.
The wealthy surfeit of their wealth,
Grudging the ploughman's strength and health.
The man, who weds the loveliest wife,
Weds, with her loveliness, much strife.
One wants an heir: another rails
Upon his heirs and the entails.
Another—but can'st thou discern
Envies and jealousies that burn?
Bid them avaunt! and say you have
Blessings unknown, which others crave.
  "Where is the turnspit? Bob is gone,
And dinner must be drest by one:
Where is that cur—(and I am loth
To say that Betty swore an oath)—
The sirloin's spoiled; I'll give it him!"—
And Betty did look fierce and grim.
Bob, who saw mischief in her eye,
Avoided her—approaching nigh;
He feared the broomstick, too, with physics
As dread as Betty's metaphysics.
  "What star did at my birth preside,
That I should be born-slave?" he sighed:

" To tread that spit, of horrid sound—
Inglorious task—to which no hound,
That ever I knew, was abased.
Whence is my line and lineage traced?
I would that I had been professed
A lap-dog, by some dame caressed:
I would I had been born a spaniel,
Sagacious nostrilled, and called Daniel:
I would I had been born a lion,
Although I scorn a feline scion:
I would I had been born of woman,
And free from servitude—as human;
My lot had then been, I discern, fit,
And not, as now, a wretched turnspit."
    An ox replied, who heard this whine:
" Dare you at partial fate repine?
Behold me, now beneath the goad,
And now beneath the waggon's load;
Now ploughing the tenacious plain,
And housing now the yellow grain.
Yet I without a murmur bear
These various labours of the year.
Yet come it will, the day decreed
By fates, when I am doomed to bleed:
And you, by duties of your post,
Must turn the spit when I must roast;
And to repay your currish moans
Will have the pickings of my bones."
    The turnspit answered : " Superficial
Has been my gaze on poor and rich, all.
What, do the mighty ones then bear
Their load of carking grief and care?

And man perhaps—ah, goodness knows!—
May have his share of pains and woes."
   So saying, with contented look,
Bob wagged his tail, and followed cook.

———

FABLE LXVI.

The Raven, Sexton, and Worm.

(To Laura.)

My Laura, your rebukes are prudish;
For although flattery is rudish,
Yet deference, not more than just,
May be received without disgust.
Am I a privilege denied
Assumed by every tongue beside?
And are you, fair and feminine,
Prone to reject a verse benign?
And is it an offence to tell
A fact which all mankind knows well?
Or with a poet's hand to trace
The beaming lustre of your face?
Nor tell in metaphor my tale,
How the moon makes the planets pale?
I check my song; and only gaze,
Admiring what I may not praise.
   If you reject my tribute due,
I'll moralise—despite of you.
To moralise a theme is duty:
My muse shall moralise of beauty.

Amidst the galaxy of fair,
Who do not moralise, the ear
Might be offended to be told
That beauty ever can grow old.
Though you by age must lose much more
Than ever beauty lost before,
You will regard it, when 'tis flown,
As if it ne'er had been your own.
Were you by Antoninus taught?
Or is it native strength of thought,
To view with such an equal mind
The fleeting bloom to doom consigned.
Those eyes, in truth, are only clay:
As diamonds, e'en so are they.
And what is beauty in her power?
The tyrant of the passing hour.
How baseless is all human pride?
Naught have we whereon to confide.
Why lose we life in anxious cares,
And lay up hoards for future years?
Or can they cheer the sick, or buy
One hour of breath to those who die?
For what is beauty but a flower,
Grass of the field, which lives its hour?
And what of lordly man the sway,
The tyrant of the passing day?
The laws of nature hold their reign
O'er man throughout her whole domain.
The monarch of long regal line
Possesses dust as frail as mine:
Nor can he any more than I
Fever or restless pains defy.

Nor can he, more than I, delay
The mortal period of his day.
   Then let my muse remember aye
Beauty and grandeur still are clay.
The king and beggar in the tomb
Commingling in the dust and doom.
   Upon a venerable yew,
Which in the village churchyard grew,
Two ravens sat. With solemn croak
Thus to his mate a raven spoke :—
   " Ah! ah! I scent upon the blast
The odour of some flesh at last.
Huzza! it is old Dobbin's steed,
On which we daintily shall feed.
I know the scent of divers courses,
And own the present as a horse's."
   A sexton, busy at his trade,
Paused, to hear more, upon his spade ;
For death was puzzled in his brain
With sexton fees and sexton gain.
   He spoke, and said : " You blundering fowls,
Nought better in your scent than owls :
It is the squire of Hawthorn Hall,
Who now is lying under pall.
I dig his grave ;—a pretty bit
Of work it is—though I say it.
A horse's ! Ah! come out of that ;
Yet needs must own that squire was fat.
What then ? Do you birds make pretence
To smelling—which is a fifth sense—
And yet your sense of smell so coarse is
You can't distinguish man and horse's ? "

"I," said the bird, "did not intend
To do you disrespect, my friend:
Indeed, we no reflection meant
By such similitude of scent.
The Arabs—epicures—will feed,
Preferring it to all, on steed;
As Britons, of your proper brood,
Think venison to be mighty good.

The sexton roared with indignation,
And spoke, methinks, about salvation;
At any rate, his rage to carry on,
He called the ravens brutes and carrion!
The situation of the foes
Prevented they should come to blows;
But for revilings vile, as friends—
They banded words, to gain their ends.

"Hold!" said the raven, "human pride
Cannot by reason be defied.
The point is knotty; tastes may err:
Refer it to some connoisseur."

And, as he spoke, a worm unrolled
His monstrous volumes from the mould;
They chose him for the referee,
And on the pleadings they agree.

The earthworm, with a solemn face,
Reviewed the features of the case:
"For I," said he, "have doubtless dined
On carcases of every kind;
Have fed on man, fowl, beast, and fish,
And know the flavour of each dish.
A glutton is the worst: for the rest
'Tis difficult to tell the best.

If I were man, I would not strive
Upon this question,—man alive!
With other points to win applause:
The King who gives his people laws
Unto the people, who obey them;
And, though at last Death comes to slay them,
Yet were the noble souls and good
Never resigned to worms for food.
Virtue distinguishes mankind,—
Immortal is the soul and mind;
And that, which is not buried here,
Mounts somewhere; but I know not where!
So good man sexton, since the case
Appears with such a dubious face,
Excuse me, if I can't determine
What different tastes suit different vermin!"

THE TOWN MOUSE AND THE COUNTRY MOUSE.

Æsop, Babrius, Horace, Prior,
and Pope.

Our friend Dan Prior had, you know,
A tale exactly *à propos;*
Name a town life—and, in a trice,
He had a story of two mice.
    Once on a time (so runs the fable)
A country mouse—right hospitable—
Received a town mouse at his board,
Just as a farmer might a lord.
A frugal mouse upon the whole,
Yet loved his friend, and had a soul;

Knew what was handsome, and would do 't,
On just occasion *coute qui coute.*
He brought him bacon nothing lean,
Pudding that might have pleased a Dean;
Cheese, such as men of Suffolk make,
But wished it Stilton for his sake.
Yet to his guest by no means sparing,
He munched himself the rind and paring.
Our courtier scarce could touch a bit,
But showed his breeding and his wit,
And did his best to seem to eat—
And said : " I vow you're mighty neat;
But, my dear friend, this savage scene!—
I pray you come and live with men.
Consider mice, like men, must die ;
Then crop the rosy hours that fly."

The veriest hermit in the nation
May yield, all know, to strong temptation :
Away they went, through thick and thin,
To a tall house near Lincoln's Inn.
The moonbeam fell upon the wall,
And tipped with silver roof and all,—
Palladian walls, Venetian doors,
Grotesco roofs and stucco floors;
And, let it in one word be said,
The moon was up—the men abed—
The guests withdrawn had left, though late,
When down the mice sat *tête à tête.*

Our courtier walks from dish to dish,
And tastes of flesh, and fowl, and fish;
Tells all their names, lays down the law,
  " *Que ça est bon !   Ah, goutez ça !*

That jelly's rich, this malmsey's healing,
Pray dip your whiskers and your tail in!"
Was ever such a happy swain—
He stuffs, and sips, and stuffs again!
  "I'm quite ashamed—'tis mighty rude
To eat so much—all is so good."
But as he spoke, bounce from the hall
Rushed chaplain, butler, dogs, and all.
Oh! for the heart of Homer's mice
Or gods, to save them in a trice;
It was by miracle they think,
For Roman stucco has no chink.
  "But, please your honour," said the peasant,
"This same dessert is not so pleasant :
Give me again my hollow tree,
A crust of bread, and liberty!"

The Magpie and her Brood.

*From the Tales of Bonaventura des Periers, Servant to Marguerite
of Valois, Queen of Navarre. By* Horace Lord Orford.

How anxious is the pensive parents' thought,
How blest the lot of fondlings, early taught;
Joy strings her hours on pleasure's golden twine,
And fancy forms it to an endless line.
But ah! the charm must cease, or soon or late,
When chicks and misses rise to woman's state :
The little tyrant grows in turn a slave,
And feels the soft anxiety she gave.
This truth, my pretty friend, an ancient sage,
Who wrote in tale and legend many a page,

Couch'd in that age's unaffected guise,
When fables were the wisdom of the wise.
To careless notes I've tuned his Gothic style,
Content, if you approve, and LAURA smile.

ONCE on a time a magpie led
   Her little family from home,
To teach them how to win their bread,
   When she afar would roam :
She pointed to each worm and fly,
Inhabitants of earth and sky,
   Or where the beetle buzzed, she called ;
But indications all were vain,—
They would not budge—the urchin train,
   But cawed, and cried, and squalled ;
They wanted to return to nest,
To nestle to mamma's warm breast,
And thought that she should seek the meat
Which they were only born to eat—
   But Madge knew better things :
" My loves," said she, " behold the plains,
Where stores of food, where plenty reigns ;
I was not half so big as you,
When me my honoured mother drew
   Forth to the groves and springs—
She flew away, before aright
I knew to read or knew to write,
   Yet I made shift to live :
So must you too—come, hop away—
Get what you can—steal what you may,
   For industry will thrive."
" But, bless us !" cried the peevish chits,
" Can babes like us live by our wits ?

With perils compassed round, can we
Preserve our lives and liberty?
Ah! how escape the fowler's snare,
And gard'ner with his gun in air,
Who, if we pilfer plums or pears,
Will scatter lead about our ears?
And you would drop a mournful head
To see your little pies lie dead!"

  "My dears," she said, and kissed their bills,
"The wise by foresight baffle ills,
A wise descent you claim;
To bang a gun off takes some time,—
A man must load, a man must prime,
  A man must take an aim—
He lifts the tube, he shuts one eye,—
'Twill then be time enough to fly;
You, out of reach, may laugh and chatter:
To cheat a man is no great matter."

  "Ay, but "—"But what?" "Why, if the clown
Should take a stone to knock us down?"

  "Why, if he do—you flats!
Must he not stoop to raise the stone?
The stooping warns you to be gone;
  Birds are not killed like cats."

  "But, dear mamma, we yet are scared,
The rogue, you know, may come prepared
A big stone in his fist!"

  "Indeed, my darlings," Madge replies,
"If you already are so wise:
  Go, cater where you list."

THE THREE WARNINGS.

Mrs. Thrale.

The tree of deepest root is bound
With most tenacity to earth;
  'Twas therefore thought by ancient sages,
  That with the ills of life's last stages
The love of life increased, with dearth
Of fibres rooting it to ground.
  It was young Dobson's wedding-day,
Death summoned him, the happy groom,
Into a sombre private room,
  From marriage revelries away;
And, looking very grave, said he:
"Young Dobson, you must go with me."
  "Not if I know it," Dobson cried;
  "What! leave my Susan,—quit my bride?
I shan't do any such a thing;
  Besides I'm not at all prepared,—
My thoughts are all upon the wing.
  I'm not the fellow to be scared,
Old Death, by you and those pale awnings:
I have a right to my three warnings."
And Death, who saw that of the jobs on
His hand, just then, tough was this Dobson,
  Agreed to go and come again;
So, as he re-adjusted awnings
  About his brows, agreed three warnings
    Should be allowed; and Dobson, fain

K

To go back to the feast, agreed
Next time to do as was decreed:
And so they parted, with by-byes,
And "humble servants," "sirs," and "I's."
   And years ran by right cheerily:
Susan was good, and children three,—
All comforts of his days—they reared;
So Dobson tumbled, unawares,
Upon the bourn of fourscore years,
   And Death then reappeared—
And Dobson said, with look of wonder,
"Holloa, old Death—another blunder!
   You may go back again: you see
   You promised me three warnings—three;
      Keep word of honour, Death!"
"Ay, ay," said Death, and raised his veil,
"I'm joyed to see you stout and hale;
I'm glad to see you so well able
To stump about from farm to stable,
   All right in limb and breath."
"So, so—so, so!"—old Dobson sighed—
"A little lame though." Death replied:
"Ay, lame; but then you have your sight?"
   But Dobson said—"Not quite, not quite."
"Not quite; but still you have your hearing?"
But Dobson said, "Past all repairing,
   Ears gone downright!"
Death on his brow then dropped the awnings,
And said—"Friend you can't stay behind:
If you are lame, and deaf, and blind,
You have had your three sufficient warnings."

POSTSCRIPT.

THE moralist, my dear niece, has said that—
> "The man of sense will read a work of note
> In the like humour as the author wrote."

To which end we must try to identify the reign of King George I. and the manners of that era with these fables; for manners change with every age, and every age has its transitions of political and social manners:

> "Manners with fortunes, humours turn with climes,
> Tenets with books, and principles with times."

It was in the era of the two first Georges that Gay wrote and applied these fables, filled with diatribes against ministers, courtiers, and misers, and inveighing against court corruption and bribery.

It was a period of transition, such as had before occurred, from feudal to monarchial, and now from monarchial to ministerial rule. We had entered into another phase—one of civil and religious liberty; but, at the same time, the royal court was a scene devoid of any graces: the kings could not speak our language, and their feminine favourites were the reverse of fair or virtuous; whilst domestic hate ruled in the palace. Power then ran into a new groove of corruption and bribery; and the scene, vile in itself, was made viler by exaggeration and the retaliations of one political party on the other, whilst either side was equally lauded by its own party. Therefore we may reasonably conclude that matters were not so bad as they were painted, and moreover that it was but a change and transition of evils, to play a part and disappear. The advent of the third George to the throne, and the rigid integrity of the first and second Pitt, reversed the story as read in these fables; the court became pure, the king true, the ministers honest, and the nation progressed from the miserable peace of Utrecht, in 1714, to the proud position we held on its centenary at Vienna, in 1814. We may grant, then, that Gay had reason on his side when he inveighed so bitterly against courts and kings; and, granting that, we may recognise the amelioration of the court of the present day, wholly free from corruption and presenting a school to be followed rather than contemned.

In the fable of the 'Degenerate Bees,' Gay takes the part of the Tory ministry,—Oxford, Bolingbroke, Dean Swift, and Mat. Prior; and in the 'Ant in Office' he alludes to a Whig minister of that day. We must not be too hard on ministers. Kings and the nation have been open to bribes and assenting to French diplomacy,—

"When policy regained what arms had lost."

Louis XI. purchased the retreat of Edward IV. in 1475, when he seized on the domains of King Réné—Provence, Anjou, Maine, Touraine, and Lorraine, and Burgundy from the domains of Charles the Bold; when we abandoned our blood allies for bribes. Again, in 1681, Charles II. was the pensioner of Louis XIV., when Louis seized on Strasbourg. William III. reluctantly let it pass at the peace and treaty of Ryswick, which Louis dictated; and it was very basely abandoned by us at the peace of Utrecht, in 1714, when we abandoned our ally the emperor, and the degenerate Bees of the fable suffered exile and the Tower, barely escaping death from the indignant nation. Again, in the treaty of Vienna, 1814, we sacrificed the interests of Austria to France, in ceding to the latter the pillaged counties of the Messin and of Alsace. Finding, therefore, like results from wholly different causes, we must not be extreme to judge, but, with Gay, admit the ministers of 1714 to grace, for they only then did what we sanctioned in 1814, and which 1870 sees righted, and the German towns restored to Germany.

I am now rounding off half a century in which I have wandered in this wilderness of a world, and in all that time I have never known, or heard of, corruption in a minister of state.   I have seen and known many fall untimely to ministerial labours and responsibility.   Walking through the streets and squares we may behold the noble brows of Pitt, Canning, Lord George Bentinck, Sir Robert Peel, Lord Palmerston—men " on whose brows shame is ashamed to sit "—and, we might add, another Canning, a Follett, Sir George Lewis, and a hecatomb of Colonial rulers, who have died, overtasked by toil and responsibility; but in all that time we have never heard a minister accused of corruption, or building palaces, or making a fortune from public treasure. Corruption, if so it may still be termed, has taken another phase; it has bowed its head and courted democracy, like to the Roman king, Ancus Martius, "nimium gaudens popu- laribus auris"—cringing to popular suffrage—to ride into place and power, by granting measures momentarily floating uppermost, and suffering the tail to guide the head, as did the snake in Æsop's fable.   We attained the height of grandeur of 1814 under the guidance of the head, and we are now upon our trial of democratical government, and whether it be equal to the old.   Under such auspices commerce has been the petted minion of the last thirty years. Not the native forest tree of Pitt, Huskisson, and Canning, but the hot-bed plant of the advocates of a predominant trade. No British statesman ever dreamt of restricting commerce, —which ever was the bond of unity of nations; but we have sunk every interest at home to swell the exports and imports, to make Britain what **Egypt** was in the days of the patriarch—the **storehouse of the** world. Egypt and England both put their agriculturists to pain, and the rural population to serfdom; but they only **exchange** the stable basis of well-being for an unstable one, for commerce is proverbially of a fleeting nature.

The age in which Gay wrote was eminently what we now designate as conservative. Excise was hateful then; as customs are denounced now, so home taxation was denounced then. So wonderfully do systems change, that in the monthly table of the revenue of this period (December, 1870), the customs do not raise one-third of the revenue, of which the other two-thirds are raised by home taxation.

From ministers proceed we to the misers. I doubt whether any domestic changes have wrought so great an amelioration in our well-being as banks and banking. It has saved us from burglars; it has, by cheques, redeemed us from the tyranny of tradesmen's books. It has put personal property on a stronger foundation than it held, and the banker keeps an excellent private account, gratuitously, of your receipts and expenditure. The trouble that the possession of gold gave to its possessor before this wonderful institution was brought to bear, may be told by a few instances of divers epochs. There is a tale of a man who was supposed to have discovered the treasures of Crœsus, in the treasury—such as is shown now at Mycenæ and Orchomenos as the treasuries of old. The hero of the tale having discovered the crypt and its hoard, built another, and spent half of his life in secretly removing the treasures of Crœsus to his new treasury; which was no sooner a deed accomplished than he perceived the original treasury was superior to the new, and he spent an equal amount of years in secretly restoring the treasures to their original crypt, where doubtless they are now, for he died whilst he was the slave to the gold. Herodotus has stories quite as marvellous as this, of the fortunate finder of the treasures of Crœsus. But our friend Mr. Pepys—who, I believe, has given us more amusement than any other Englishman, be he whom he may—is more amusing and instructive. His story is written in 1667, the year after the fire of London, and whilst the invasion of the Dutch was apprehended, and we will see how Mr. Pepys fulfilled the adage of " as much trouble as all my money." On 30th March, 1666, we find him write :—" I to Lombard St., and there received 2200*l*., and brought it home, and, contrary to expectation, received 35*l*. for the use of 2000*l*. of it for a quarter of a year, where it hath produced me this profit, and hath been a conveniency to me as to care and security at my house, and demandable at two days' warning, as this has been."

On 12th November :—" This day I received 450 pieces of gold, which cost me 22½*d*. change. But I am well contented with it, I having now nearly 2800*l*. in gold, and will not rest till I get full 3000*l*." But on the 13th June, 1667, on the sad news of the taking of the ' Royal Charles,' and sinking ships at Barking Creek, " put me into such a fear, that I presently resolved of my father's and wife's going into the country ; and at two hours' warning they did go by the coach this day with 1300*l*. in gold in their night-bag. Pray God give them good passage, and good care to hide it when they come home ! But my heart is full of fear. They gone, I continued in frights and fear what to do with the rest."

And on the 10th October, when the Dutch were gone, we read :—" Up, and to walk up and down in the garden with

my father, to talk of all our concernments : about a **husband**
for my sister, whereof there is at **present no** appearance ; but
we must endeavour **to** find her one **now,** for she grows old
and **ugly.** My **father** and **I** with **a dark** lantern, **it** being
now light, into the **garden with my** wife, and there went
about our **great work** to dig **up my gold.** But, Lord, what a
tosse **I was for** some **time in, that they** could not justly tell
where it **was** : but by-and-bye, poking **with a** spit, we found
it, and then began with **a spudd. But,** good God ! to see
how **sillily they did it, not** half **a foot** under ground, and in
the sight of the world from **a** hundred **places, and** within
sight of a neighbour's window. Only **my father** says that he
saw **them all gone to church before** he began the work when
he laid the money. But I was **out of my** wits almost, and
the more from **that,** upon my lifting the earth with my spudd,
I did discern **that I had scattered the** pieces of gold in the
loose earth, and, **taking up the** iron head-pieces whereon
they **were put, I perceived the earth had** gotten among the
gold, and **wet, so that the bags were all** rotten and notes ; so
that **I could not tell what in the world to** say to it, not
knowing **how to judge what was wanting, or what** had been
lost by Gibson in **his journey down,** which, **all put** together,
did make me mad. **And at last I was** obliged to take up the
pieces, dirt **and all, by candle-light, and** carry them into my
brother's **chamber, and there lock** them up, whilst **I eat** a
little supper ; **and then, all** people going to bed, William
Hewer and I did, all alone, with pails of water and besoms,
wash the dirt off **the pieces,** and then began to tell them, by
a note which **I had of the value of** the whole in my pocket,
and do find that **there** was short above **a** hundred pieces,
which **did** make me **mad. . . . .** So William Hewer and I
out again **about** midnight, and there **by** candle-light did

make shift to gather forty pieces more; and so to bed, and there lay in some disquiet until daylight. 11th.—And then William Hewer and I, with pails and a sieve, did lock ourselves into the garden, and did gather the earth and then sift those pails in one of the summer-houses (just as they do for diamonds in other parts), and there, to our great content did, by nine o'clock, make the last night's forty-five up to seventy-nine; so that we are come to some twenty or thirty of what I think the true number should be. So do leave my father to make a second examination of the dirt, and my mind at rest on it, being but an accident; and so give me some kind of content to remember how painful it is sometimes to keep money as well as to get it, and how doubtful I was to keep it all night, and how to secure it to London.

"About ten o'clock, took coach, my wife and I, and Willett and W. Hewer, and Mumford and Bowles (whom my lady sent me to go along with me my journey, not telling her the reason, but it was only to secure my gold), and my brother John on horseback; and with these four I thought myself pretty safe. My gold I put into a basket, and set it under one of the seats; and so my work every quarter of an hour was to look to see whether all was well; and I did ride in great fear all the day. 12th.—By five o'clock got home, and did bring my gold to my heart's content very safe, having not this day carried it in a basket, but in our hands; the girl took care of one, and my wife of another bag, and I the rest, I being afraid of the bottom of the coach lest it should break." Such is Mr. Pepys' story.

"Nor light nor darkness brings his pains relief:
   One shows the plunder, and one hides the thief."

Mr. Crabbe has portrayed the marvel of an honest inhabitant of Aldborough, when first he learnt, in his graphic phrase, "that money would breed,"—that it could afford to pay yearly interest. Shakespeare has several references to the fact. Shylock, and a clown in ' Twelfth Night ' making very quaint allusions. I shall only add one more tale from Mr. S. Trench's late stories of ' Realities of Irish Life.' A neighbour, who had saved two hundred pounds in gold, kept it in the thatch of his roof. One day he appeared before Mr. Trench bearing his gold, and requesting him to be his depositee, expressing the comfort it would afford him. Mr. Trench declined the unprofitable duty, and pointed out to him the bank, which would accept his deposit and give him interest. The eye of Patrick flashed with intelligence and foresight as he warned Mr. Trench from the delusion of banks, which every year wasted the original sum by paying the stipend, and when you wished to reclaim the original, lo, it had disappeared. No, no, he would have no dividend, forsooth, to eat away his capital ; which he bore back again (about five pounds' weight) and replaced it in his thatch. It was neither lost nor wasted there ; it became the inheritance of his only daughter, a woman of extreme energy, who had from childhood loved--more, methinks, as a mother loves a helpless child—a good-hearted, unvicious piece of indolence and sloth. She followed him to New York and married him, nolens volens ; and Providence assigned to him an energetic woman, to make his castle of indolence a bed of roses to the satisfaction of them both,—supplying for each the energy and the repose, both constitutional, both unvicious, which the other lacked.

Highwaymen beset the highways, as burglars invaded the residences ; and Macaulay chuckles over the fact that his bête noire—the noble Marlborough—was cased of 5000l. in gold in one of his trips between London and St. Alban's.

From the regions of ministers and misers we may descend to the equally disputed realms of the muses. Horace terms it " the peevish and inhuman muse," which those who drink of Aganippe's fountain woo; whilst others are apt to equal their Castalian spring and Parnassus with the height of the empyreal, regarding with pity the toilers on the land and deep. But herein, as in aught else, it is the mind, and not the outward circumstances, which makes the happiness suited to its strength and position; for it must be confessed it is from the weak in bodily frame, the lame, and the blind, that we draw our poets; and when we find a rare bodily exception to the rule, we find too often a mind insatiate of applause, and pining for more appreciation of their productions. The votaries of the muse cannot be set down as so happy and contented as many a ploughman, nor does the smoothness of, the lines gratify the eye more than the smoothness of the furrow. But these rhymes of Gay hardly aspire to the height of poesy, nor do they possess the banter and raciness, such as we find in Butler's 'Hudibras' :—

> " When oyster-women lock their fish up,
>   And trudge away to bawl, 'No bishop!'"

Neither has it the deep pathos of the Spenserian stanza, which perhaps strives at the deepest vein of poetry. Take two of Thomson's, for example :—

> " O mortal man, who livest here by toil,
>   Do not complain of this thy hard estate;
>   That like an emmet thou must ever moil,
>   Is a hard sentence of an ancient date:
>   And, certes, there is for it reason great;
>   For though sometimes it makes thee weep and wail,
>   And curse thy star, and early drudge and late,
>   Withouten that would come a heavier bale,—
>   Loose life, unruly passions, and diseases pale."

And another stanza runs thus :—

" I care not, Fortune, what you me deny :
    You cannot rob me of free Nature's grace ;
    You cannot shut the windows of the sky,
    Through which Aurora shows her brightening face ;
    You cannot bar my constant feet to trace
    The woods and lawns by living stream at eve.
    Let health my nerves and finer fibres brace,
    And I their toys to the great children leave ;
    Of fancy, reason, virtue, nought can me bereave."

Such is the *stanza* in which are written Spenser's 'Faërie
Queen,' Thomson's 'Castle of Indolence,' and Byron's
'Childe Harold,' and it is the highest flight of poetry : after
which comes the heroic verse, in which we lap the heavy
poems we call epic—their Latin appellation; of these the
Iliads of Homer and the Æneids of Virgil are the ever
recurring aspirations of poets doomed to fall untimely.
The charm of Homer is that it is not only a poem, but it
instructs us in the history—all that we know of it—of those
prehistoric days. It is full of ballads, which are the ground-
work by which we trace the manners and the tenets of the
pagan tribes. The truth involved in 'Homer' is the charm
of his epic poem, while the falsehood involved in the
'Henriade' of Voltaire is amply sufficient to condemn it
utterly. For a specimen let us take Pope's 'Homer,' where
Hector answers Andromache's appeal to stay and guard the
walls of Troy :—

" The chief replied, 'That post shall be my care;
    Nor that alone, but all the works of war;
    Still foremost let me stand to guard the throne,
    To save my father's honours and my own :
    Yet come it will, the day decreed by Fates—
    How my heart trembles whilst my tongue relates—

That day when thou, imperial Troy, must bend,
Must see thy warriors fall, thy glories end.
And yet no presage dire so wounds my mind—
My mother's death, the ruin of my kind—
As thine, Andromache, thy griefs I dread.
I see thee weeping, trembling, captive led,
In Argive looms our battles to design,
Woes—of which woes so large a part was thine;
To bear the victor's hard commands, or bring
The waters from the Hypercian spring.
There, whilst you groan beneath the load of life,
They cry " Behold the Trojan Hector's wife!"
Some Argive, who shall live thy griefs to see,
Embitters thy great woe by naming me:
The thoughts of glory past and present shame,
A thousand griefs, shall waken at the name.
May I lie cold before that dreadful day,
Pressed by a load of monumental clay
Thy Hector, wrapped in everlasting sleep,
Shall neither hear thee sigh nor see thee weep.' "

Next in pathos is the *mournful* elegy; of which none can surpass Gray's elegy :—

" The boast of heraldry, the pomp of power,
And all that beauty, all that wealth e'er gave,
Alike await the inevitable hour;
The paths of glory lead but to the grave.

Can storied urn or animated bust
Back to its mansion call the fleeting breath?
Can honour's voice provoke the silent dust,
Or flattery soothe the dull cold ear of death?

Full many a gem of purest ray serene
The dark unfathomed caves of ocean bear;

Full many a flower is born to blush unseen,
And waste its sweetness on the desert air.

Let not ambition mock our useful toil,
Our homely joys and destiny obscure,
Nor grandeur hear with a disdainful smile
The short and simple annals of the poor :

Their names, their years spelt by the untaught Muse,
The place of fame and elegy supply,
And many a holy text around she strews,
To teach the rustic moralist to die."

Nursery rhymes, old ballads, odes, sonnets, epigrams, travesties, fables, satires, and eclogues, and, most of all, songs, provide daily pleasure for us from our cradle to the grave. Every language has its nursery rhymes, which are a sort of Delphian lot, sung in enigma from 'King Pittacus of Mytilene' and 'Le bon Roi Dagobert,' to the lullaby of 'Four-and-twenty Blackbirds.' There is as much sarcasm in nursery rhymes as there is of pride and boast in the songs of bards at the feast of heroes, and as there is of humble confession in the funeral psalm. Song tends alike to evaporate exuberant spirits, and to soothe the soul in an affliction—as Desdemona informs us so sweetly in her misery :—

" My mother had a maid called Barbara ;
She was in love : and he she loved proved mad,
And did forsake her. She had a song of willow,
An old thing 'twas ; but it expressed her fortune,
And she died singing it. That song to-night
Will not go from my mind : I have much to do,
But to go hang my head all of one side,
And sing it like poor Barbara."

Ophelia chanted as she floated down the brook, Arion tamed the flood, and Orpheus the trees and rocks. It is a marvellous power which soothes alike the babe in the arms and the hero at the feast, the lover and the forsaken maiden, which leads to battle and returns from conquest; therefore let us see the ODE, in ' Eton Revisited ' :—

" Ah, happy hills ! ah, pleasing shade !
  Ah, fields beloved in vain !
Where once my careless boyhood stra
  A stranger yet to pain.
I feel the gales that from ye blow
A momentary bliss bestow,
  As waving fresh their gladsome wing
My weary soul they seem to soothe,
And redolent of joy and youth,
  To breathe a second spring.

Whilst some on earnest labour bent
  Their business, murmuring, ply
'Gainst graver hours that bring constraint
  To sweeten liberty ;
✚ Some bold adventurers disdain
  The limits of the little reign
And unknown regions dare descry ;
  Still as they run they look behind,
  And hear a voice in every wind,
And snatch a fearful joy.

To each his sufferings, all are men
  Condemned alike to groan ;
The tender, for another's pain—
  The unfeeling, for his own.
Yet, ah ! why should they know their fate,
Since sorrow never comes too late ;
And happiness too swiftly flies ?

Thought would destroy their paradise.
No more : ' where ignorance is bliss,
'Tis folly to be wise.' "

Let me add four lines from Denham's poem, ' On Cooper's Hill,' addressing the River Thames :—

"O could I flow like thee, and make thy stream
My great example, as it is my theme!
Though deep yet clear, though gentle yet not dull,
Strong without rage, without o'erflowing full."

Our old ballads are very fine : the opening of ' Chevy Chase ' is equal to ' Wrath, Goddess sing the Wrath of Achilles,' or ' Arms and the Man :'—

" The Persé owt of Northumberland,
And a vowe to Godde made he,
That he would hunt in the mountains
Of Cheviot within days three.
In maugre of doughty Douglas
And all that ever with him be,
The fattest hartes in all Cheviot,
He said, to kill and bear away.
' By my faith!' quoth the doughty Douglas then,
' I will lette that hunting, gif I may.'

Worde is commen to Eddenburrowe
To James, the Scottish King,
That doughty Douglas, Lyfftenant of Marches,
Lay slain Chevyot hills within.
His handdès did James weal and wryng,
Sighing, ' Alas! and woe is me—
Such another captain Scotland within
I trow there will never be!'
Worde is còmmen to lovely Londone
Till the fourth Harry, our King,

That Lord Persé, Lyfftenant of Marches,
Lay slain Cheviot hills within.
'God have mercy on his soul!' said Kyng Harry,
'Good Lord, if thy will it be.
I have a hondrith Captains in Englonde
As good as ever was he;
But Persé, and I brook my lyffe
Thy death well quit shall be.'
This was the honting off the Cheviot
'That tear beganne this spurn:'
Old men that known the ground well enough
Call it the battle of Otterburn.
At Otterburn began this spurn
Upon a Monnynday;
There was the doughtie Douglas slain,
The Persé went captive away."

But of every species of poetry none are so rife with life and beauty as the song. It conjoins music with words, and brevity with sweetness. There is no position in which man does not sing,—in joy to express it, and in woe to relieve it : in company in chorus, and alone for companionship. Sir Walter Scott has imagined the minstrel to sing :—

"I have song of war for knight,
    Lay of love for ladye bright,
    Fairie tale to lull the heir,
    Goblin grim the maid to scare.
    If you pity kith or kin,
    Take the wandering harper in."

But songs are like the flowers of the field : each age hath its own, which fade and perish and make way for another crop, and every age claims its own. For melody, terseness, and beauty of words, the song excels more than any other form

L

of poetry ; and they are wise who have a private collection of the songs which, like swallows, come and disappear.

It may appear strange to print the Fables of Gay, and say no word of our author ; but the truth is that it is unkind to withdraw the veil of privacy from any man's life. Doctor Johnson did an unkind deed when he wrote the 'Lives of the Poets;' for which he was fully repaid when Boswell flayed him bare as ever Apollo flayed Marsyas, and exposed all the quivering nerves to the light of day. Of all classes of men, the class of poets most need the concealing veil : the greatest have been blind ; the next greatest halt, and the remainder weak or deformed of frame. Debarred the healthier paths of life, man rushes for employment to the refuging muse ; and rightly so, for he finds an employment ornamental and useful still. But solitude does not nurture the virtues of the soul more than physical defect does that of the body, and the withdrawal of the curtain divulges a very sad sight of discontent and envy. Homer himself is recorded to have ejaculated his aspiration to be the favourite of the Greek girls and boys. A poet seer loves no brother near his throne, and is but too apt to complain of non-appreciation of his muse on the part of the world. The fault rather is in their own too sensitive souls ; and it is a fact that there is scarcely a name in the roll of poets, whose fame is not harmed by divulging his exotic life. The rural labourer's fate—

"Where to be born and die,
Of rich and poor, make all the history"—
is far better than to be paraded from the disobedience of youth, the rebellion of manhood, and the disappointment of age, divulged in the storied lives of the few hundred names admitted to be British poets ; and the reading of whose works

is, as a rule, a task of weariness. The career of Gay is a very fair one as an average of the poetic. He mainly avoided the enumerated ills—enumerated by Dr. Johnson—

"Toil, envy, want, the patron, and the jail."

The poetic element in Britain was very strong in the days of Gay. Pope, Swift, Prior, Addison were the petted servants of the Ministers. They were all far more successful in their careers than was Gay, who from his boyhood refused to labour for his bread. Very early he found a patroness in the Duchess of Monmouth, who had

"Wept over Monmouth's bloody tomb,"

with whom he enjoyed a sort of honorary post—secretary to the shadow of a princess; next he became a real secretary to the Earl of Clarendon, Ambassador at Hanover, as Prior had been to the Ambassador at Paris. We easily trace in Gay's career the unsatisfied overweening poetic soul, like a Charybdis, insatiable of adulation. In 1716, the Earl of Burlington cheered him at his seat in Devon; in 1717, he accompanied Mr. Pulteney to Aix; in 1718, Lord Harcourt soothed his spirits. Then he made money, which burnt holes in his pockets. He called his friends together, to ask how he should invest. His poetic friends Pope and Swift advised him to sink it in an annuity. But fate or fortune cast him in with Secretary Craggs and the South Sea scheme, and, from the possessor of 20,000*l.*, his capital collapsed to *nil*. In vain he had been bidden to sell and to realize. He had visions of wealth, and held on to be accidentally an honester man than if he had enriched himself by that delusive scheme; but he nearly sunk beneath his disappointment, and his health was endangered. Hope and the Muse restored him to more life and to more disappointment. He then wrote 'The Captive,' obtained an appointment to read it to the Princess of Wales, stumbled, like Cæsar, over a stool; the princess screamed, the omen was a true one—'The Captive' pined and died.

In 1726 he wrote these Fables, dedicating them to the Duke of Cumberland, and in 1727 his royal patron succeeded to the crown; when he was offered the post of Gentleman Usher to the Princess Louisa. Gay was hurt and indignant, and made court to Mrs. Howard (afterwards Countess of Suffolk), one of the anomalous favourites alluded to in page 131, but in vain.

Then came the great success of his 'Beggars' Opera,' which was followed by 'Polly,' its sequel. 'Polly' was forbidden by the Lord Chamberlain, and a private subscription raised 1200*l.* to recompense Gay for not being suffered to please the mob with his immorality. And, lastly, the Duke and Duchess of Queensberry took this child of nature by the hand—the duke to manage his worldly substance, and the duchess to soothe his insatiable vanity—and so he died at the early age of 45, and has a very pretty tomb, with " Queensberry weeping o'er his urn," in Poets' Corner. Pope's epitaph runs thus :—

" Blest be the gods for those they took away,
   And those they left me, for they left me Gay.
Left me to see deserted genius bloom,
   Neglected die, and tell it on his tomb;
Of all his blameless life the sole return
   My verse and Queensberry weeping o'er his urn."

Peace with his dust! Another couplet of Pope's, methinks, has more of moral truth and justice :—

" A wit's a feather, and a chief's a rod;
   An honest man 's the noblest work of God."

LONDON : PRINTED BY WILLIAM CLOWES AND SONS, STAMFORD STREET,
AND CHARING CROSS.